Flip-Flops
and
Murder

BAREFOOT SLEUTH MYSTERIES

BOOK ONE

H.Y. HANNA

CONTENTS

CHAPTER ONE

"MIND THE GAP! DOORS... CLOSING..."

Ellie Bishop raced for the platform just as the shrill *beep-beep-beep* signal sounded, warning of the train doors closing. She hopped on board with a second to spare and sagged against the wall with a sigh of relief. If she had missed this train, she would probably have had to wait another ten minutes before another one came past the station.

That was the problem with living in the outer suburbs. If she had been at one of the stations in central London, there would have been a lot more trains, especially at this time of the morning rush hour. But Ellie didn't have much choice: last month, instead of producing the ring that she had been expecting, her boyfriend of three years had instead confessed that he had been seeing someone else behind her back. Ellie had stormed out of their shared apartment and—with minimal savings and no place of her own—had been forced to move back in with her parents.

Still, she should hardly complain, she admitted. After all, she was lucky to have parents who were happy to take her in, and their home was a comfortable townhouse in a respectable, middle-class neighborhood. But ask any twenty-something and they'll tell you that it's pretty tough moving back to live with your parents when you've been used to your independence. Especially when your parents didn't approve of your life choices!

Ellie sighed as she thought of the argument she'd had at breakfast with her parents that morning:

"When are you going to get a real job?" her father had asked.

"What d'you mean? I do have a real job," Ellie answered. "I'm a receptionist at a publishing company."

"A *temporary* receptionist," said her father, glowering at her. "This is the sixth temp job you've had this year."

"Temping is a very respectable way of earning money," said Ellie defensively.

"It's not a career, dear. There's no stability," her mother complained, passing the butter. "You need a job that will give you security—the kind that your father and I have."

Ellie pulled a face. The last thing she wanted was

to be a banker like her father or a teacher like her mother. Sure, they were respectable, stable jobs, but she couldn't think of anything more boring.

"Look at your sister…" her mother had continued and Ellie had swallowed a sigh. She should have known that her parents would bring Karen up at some point. Her elder sister was the poster child for "responsible adulthood." Still just in her early thirties, Karen had already achieved a senior position in a reputable law firm, was happily married, and had two well-behaved, beautifully groomed children in an elite primary school. Her life was balanced, secure, and mapped out to the last minute.

Now, as Ellie leaned against the side of the train, she grimaced again as she thought of her sister. Karen was everything that she was not and could never hope to be. *Nor do I want to be!* Ellie thought mutinously. She sighed as she turned to look out of the train window. There was nothing to see, of course, except the walls of the tunnel as the train rattled through London's underground system. The darkened windows reflected her own face back at her and Ellie stared at her reflection: the small snub nose with its smattering of freckles, the generous mouth and wide brown eyes, and the tangle of curly brown hair which refused to be tamed no matter how much she tried with straightening tongs. She knew she didn't have the kind of face that could grace fashion magazines, the kind of face that belonged to models who traveled the world and visited exotic places…

and yet that was exactly the kind of life she yearned for.

Well, maybe not travelling the world, but at least travelling somewhere away from London, thought Ellie with a wistful sigh.

While her parents wanted her to settle down to a safe, stable job, what *she* really wanted was adventure: the chance to live in another country, experience another culture, learn new things, meet new people; to feel that there was more to life than just this nine-to-five grind.

The train stopped at another station and the doors flew open. Ellie was jostled and shoved against the wall of the compartment as more commuters piled in with their bulky winter coats and heavy bags and knapsacks. The windows began steaming up with all the bodies inside and Ellie wrinkled her nose at the smell of damp wool mixed with hair spray, deodorant, and various other odors that resulted from human bodies packed close together. She closed her eyes and imagined herself on a beautiful beach instead, with sparkling blue water, white sand between her toes, and a breeze blowing gently through nearby palm trees... the fragrance of plumeria... the warmth of sunshine on her face...

"DOORS... CLOSING... *Beep-beep-beep-beep—*"

Ellie's eyes flew open and she gasped as she realized that she had been so immersed in her daydream, she had completely missed the train arriving at her station.

"Sorry! Excuse me!" she cried, pushing her way through the crowd of bodies.

She jumped off the train just as the doors slid shut behind her, narrowly missing the hem of her coat. Breathing a sigh of relief, Ellie shouldered her bag and hurried through the station and onto the street, making her way to the small educational publisher that she worked for. The phone was already ringing when she arrived at the reception desk. Hastily, she dropped her bag on the chair and shrugged out of her coat before answering the call. For the next hour and a half, Ellie took inquiries, redirected calls to various departments, greeted visitors, and signed for deliveries. She was glad to take a break at 10:30 a.m. for morning tea. Claire, one of the secretaries, came to cover the phones for her and, even after Ellie returned from the kitchen, she hung around, obviously interested in gossip.

"Got anything nice planned for Christmas?" she asked as she moved aside for Ellie to resume her seat behind the reception desk.

Ellie shook her head. "No, not really. It's still over a month away—"

"Yeah, but you've got to have something to look forward to, don't you?" said Claire, pouting. "I hate this time of year! Everything's already getting so dark and gray and cold. Wouldn't you love to be able to go away every winter to somewhere warm and nice?"

"Of course, who wouldn't? But unless we win the lottery, that's not going to happen anytime soon," said Ellie.

"Somewhere really warm and sunny..." continued Claire dreamily. "Like the Maldives... or the Bahamas... or even Florida. Wouldn't you love to be starting each morning with a swim in lovely warm water instead of a boring commute?"

"Well, I would... if I could swim!" said Ellie with a chuckle.

"You can't swim?"

Ellie shook her head. "Never really learnt. Oh, I went with my school class for lessons at the local pool, but I hated it and never even learned to float. I always—"

She broke off as the office doors opened and a courier stepped into the reception foyer. He came up to the desk, holding an official-looking document envelope. Ellie took the clipboard he handed her and signed for it absent-mindedly. She recognized the courier as one of the regulars and smiled at him, saying, "Another one for the directors?"

"No, actually it's for..." The courier turned the envelope around to read the name on the front. "For an Elinor Bishop."

"For me?" Ellie said in surprise. Who on earth would be sending her something by DHL?

"Well, go on... open it!" said Claire eagerly after the courier had left.

Ellie slit the envelope open and drew out a sheet of hand-written letter paper, together with a printed confirmation page from a travel agency. Her eyes widened as she saw the airline logo.

"Oh my God, it's a plane ticket!" gasped Claire, leaning over Ellie's shoulder to look. "A ticket to a beach resort in Florida! You lucky cow! Who sent you that?"

Ellie shook her head in bewilderment. Then she unfolded the letter and instantly recognized the bold scrawl. It belonged to Aunt Olive, her father's much older—and much more eccentric—sister. Ellie's face broke into a smile. Aunt Olive was the only person in her family who had ever understood her. Well, it was hardly surprising considering that Aunt Olive was pretty unconventional herself. Ignoring all the usual expectations to marry, settle down, and have a family, Aunt Olive had remained a free spirit indulging in a succession of romantic liaisons until well into her forties. Then, just when everyone had thought that they couldn't be scandalized any further, she had met and married a rich American thirty years her senior. And when he died several years later, leaving her a very wealthy widow, Aunt Olive had decided to embark on a career as a mystery author. Much to the surprise of all her sneering, skeptical friends and relatives, she had become very successful and her books were now widely published and sold all over the world.

Aunt Olive also happened to be Ellie's godmother and ever since she was a little girl, Ellie had always looked forward to her aunt's visits. She didn't come to visit often but when she did, Aunt Olive always brought all sorts of wonderful gifts and fascinating games and ideas. To Ellie, her aunt had always seemed like a fairy godmother, who brought excitement and magic into her life.

And she's still doing it now, thought Ellie, grinning as she looked down at the letter in her hands. Her aunt had sent Ellie an invitation to join her in the Sunshine State.

"Dear Ellie,

I thought you might like to escape the dreary English weather for a while. So why don't you come and join me? I'm here for a writer's conference starting this weekend but I'm planning to stay on after that, spend the winter here. This resort is a fabulous place—you'd love it! You're welcome to stay as long as you like—it's my treat. Stay for Christmas and the New Year! I've got a two-room suite. Come whenever you're free. The ticket is flexible. I shall look forward to expecting you.

Your loving,
Aunt Olive"

CHAPTER TWO

"*Florida?*" Mrs. Bishop stared at Ellie in astonishment.

"Yes, Aunt Olive sent me a ticket," said Ellie. "It's flexible—I can go any time I want and it's easy to get a single seat on most flights. In fact, I rang the travel agency and checked: I can go this weekend! And Aunt Olive says I can stay as long as I like. She's planning to spend the winter there, so she's invited me to stay until the new year if I like."

"Are you mad?" asked her father, frowning at her over the top of his cereal bowl. "What about your job? You've only been working at this company for a couple of months. It's hardly the time to start gallivanting off to the other side of the world!"

"But Dad, it's not a permanent position. In fact, my temp contract ends this week. I could be looking

9

for a new temping job next week anyway."

Ellie didn't tell him that the publishing company had, in fact, offered to renew her contract. But the thought of having to spend the coming cold, dreary months behind that reception desk, when she could be in sunny Florida instead, just made her heart sink.

"I don't know what Olive is playing at," growled her father. "Sending an invitation like this to a young girl like you... She's always encouraging you in reckless behavior!"

"I think she's being very generous, Dad," Ellie protested. "I mean, it's an amazing offer. I'd be mad not to take it up! Who would turn down the chance for an all-expenses-paid holiday in Florida?"

"Yes, but life isn't just about having holidays," tutted Mr. Bishop. "What about your job? What about your career?"

"What career?" said Ellie with a shrug. "I don't really have one! You said so yourself: I've just been doing a series of temp jobs."

"Well, you'll never have one if you go running off to Florida with Olive," said her father.

"Ellie, dear, you have to remember—you're not like your aunt," said her mother in a gentler tone. "Olive is a rich widow. She doesn't have to worry about earning a living, so she can afford to treat life as a long holiday."

"Aunt Olive earns a very good living from her books," said Ellie.

"Yes, but the point is she doesn't need to," said her father. "I should know—I'm the one looking after her finances! If she never sold another book tomorrow, it wouldn't matter. She could live comfortably to the end of her days. But it's not the same for you. You haven't got a big inheritance to rely on." He looked at his daughter in exasperation. "Ellie, how many times have I told you how important it is to be financially independent?"

"Yes, I know, Dad, and I agree, but can't you try to see it from my point of view for a change? I'm only twenty-six! I've still got my whole life ahead of me, to settle down and get a stable job and whatever. I've got the chance to have an adventure now; a few more months won't matter." She gave him a persuasive smile. "I'll be back in the new year and I'll look for a proper job then—I promise. Besides, this will give me a chance to 'get it out of my system.' You know how I've always desperately wanted to travel and live somewhere overseas... Well, this is the perfect opportunity! Maybe I'll even pick up some skills that will make me even more employable when I get back."

Her father looked at her for a long moment. Finally, he sighed and leaned back in his chair. "Well, you're an adult now, Ellie, so at the end of the day, it's your decision. And yes, I suppose you're right: you *are* very lucky to have an aunt who can fund a holiday like this. I suppose it would be silly not to take advantage of the opportunity. And maybe it *would* be good for you to travel a bit, see the world—

”

"What about accommodation?" Mrs. Bishop spoke up. "Did you say you're going to be staying at a beach resort?"

Ellie nodded eagerly. "Yes! The travel agency told me about the place and I looked it up online. It's gorgeous! Right on the beach, with a huge pool and everything. It's called the Sunset Palms Beach Resort."

"And what about spending money?"

"I've got a bit of savings, and the travel agent told me that Aunt Olive's package at the resort is all-inclusive of meals and activities. So it's really shopping for some personal things, like toiletries and clothes, and I'm sure everything is cheaper in America," said Ellie blithely. "I'll be fine until the new year."

"Well, your father and I had a small amount saved up. We were planning to buy you something nice for Christmas, but seeing as you'll be off in Florida, perhaps it will be more useful if we give you the money to spend while you're there. I know your aunt is very generous and always likes to lavish gifts on you, but you mustn't abuse her generosity."

"Oh Mum!" said Ellie, surprised and touched. "Thank you! That's so sweet of you! Thanks, Mum! Thanks, Dad!" She sprang up, beaming, and hurried to hug both her parents. Then she paused and looked at them uncertainly. "Erm... you don't mind me spending Christmas and New Year there, do you? I know we normally all come back here for Christmas lunch, with Karen and Geoff and the kids, but it would just be this year—"

"That's all right, dear," said her mother with a smile. "Your father and I were actually thinking of going on a cruise. Yes, we're trying new things too! We'd seen one that we like the look of: it's a week around the Mediterranean and it looks fabulous. It departs on Boxing Day, which would mean that we'd be leaving you all the day after Christmas lunch anyway. So if you're going to be away, then that could work out very well. I'm sure Karen won't mind if we have a simpler Christmas celebration this year."

The rest of the week dragged by for Ellie. She could barely keep her mind on her work at the office. All she could think about was the upcoming trip to Florida. She had already packed and repacked her case multiple times—not that there was much to choose from in her wardrobe. Most of her nicer things were for colder weather and her shorts, tank tops, and T-shirts were all old and faded. She decided to use a bit of her recent wages to treat herself to a new summer wardrobe. So after work on Thursday, Ellie headed to Oxford Street, the main retail strip in central London, for some last-minute shopping. Unfortunately, she'd forgotten that fashion follows the seasons and since the U.K. was heading into winter, the racks were full of woolly sweaters, fleecy tops, and thick trousers. Finally, Ellie decided that she might as well wait until she got to Florida.

So she returned home empty-handed and packed the newest T-shirts she could find, along with a couple of denim skirts and shorts, and a few sundresses as well. As for her old swimming suit... Ellie examined it critically: it was faded from chlorine and the elastic along its edges was stretched and loose. She made a face and dropped it back into the drawer. She'd buy herself a nice, new bikini when she got to Florida, she decided with a smile. Something to help her get that beautiful tan she'd always wanted!

The night before her flight, Ellie could barely sleep, and by the time she was boarding the plane at London Gatwick Airport the next evening, she was nearly bursting with pent-up excitement. She had been on a plane before, of course, but only for short trips to Europe: a school trip to France, or a weekend in Spain with her ex-boyfriend. This seemed very different, very grown up, to be flying across the Atlantic.

Ellie spent most of the long flight daydreaming about her destination. She wasn't flying into Miami, as she had originally expected, but to Tampa, a bustling city on Florida's west coast, perched on the edge of the Gulf of Mexico. The travel agent had organized a car to pick her up from Tampa International Airport and take her to the resort, situated on a beach farther down the coast.

Ellie had been busy doing some online research in the evenings and she knew that the Tampa Bay area had a humid, subtropical climate, with hurricanes common in the wet season. But she was relieved to discover that November signaled the start of the dry season, with lovely, mild, sunny days and Fahrenheit temperatures rarely dipping below the sixties. When she thought of the wet and cold that she was leaving behind in London, Ellie couldn't help grinning. She couldn't wait to arrive and feel the sun on her face!

It was an overnight flight but, although she tried several times, Ellie just couldn't go to sleep. When she finally dozed off, she was woken up barely twenty minutes later by the sound of the captain's voice announcing that the plane would be landing at Tampa International Airport soon. Sitting up, Ellie rubbed her eyes and raised the window shade, looking eagerly out of the window. She was met by a vision of white clouds in a pale blue sky. It was just after 6 a.m. in Florida and the sun was creeping over the horizon.

Ellie looked down and gasped with delight as she took in the view: the dazzling blue water of Tampa Bay, with the surrounding tree-covered peninsulas extending into the bay and the occasional sandbar visible from the air. She could see channels and waterways, and beautiful little islands, and even boats like white specks in the water. Everything was so green and blue and lush and vivid... it was like looking at a postcard.

Ellie smiled to herself: *Florida, here I come!*

CHAPTER THREE

By the time Ellie had disembarked and collected her small suitcase, the adrenalin was beginning to drain away and her lack of sleep was beginning to show. She yawned and rubbed her eyes blearily as she stepped out into the Arrivals hall of the airport. There was a row of drivers holding signs waiting for passengers and Ellie's spirits lifted when she saw her own name on a white sign.

"Hi!" she said, going up to the woman holding the sign. "I think you're waiting for me?"

The woman smiled but didn't take off her black shades. "Miss Elinor Bishop?"

"Yes, that's me. But everyone calls me Ellie."

"I'm Nancy Bertoli," said the woman, holding out a hand and giving Ellie a firm handshake.

She had salt-and-pepper hair styled in a neat crop

and looked to be in her mid-fifties, with a slim, athletic figure and tanned arms. Her face seemed to be pale in comparison, though, and when she led Ellie outside to the car, she winced slightly as the sun fell on her face.

"Are you OK?" asked Ellie.

"Huh? Oh yeah... it's nothing. I'm fine," said Nancy.

She put Ellie's case in the trunk of the car, then gestured to the front passenger seat. "You want to ride in the front with me? You'll probably get a better view."

"Oh, thanks!" said Ellie, delighted. She started to walk to the left side of the car, then realized that was the driver's seat. "Oh, sorry—I forgot that you drive on the other side of the road in the States," she said with a laugh.

"Yes, and you'd better be careful when you cross the road too," said Nancy. "I've seen British tourists almost get mown down because they looked the wrong way before stepping off the curb."

"I'll look both ways," Ellie promised her.

She circled around the car to the other side and got into the front passenger seat, leaning back against the leather cushions. The resort taxi was large and comfortable, although it smelled heavily of air freshener and reminded Ellie of newly cleaned rental cars.

Nancy slid into the driver's seat beside her and reached into the back seat to retrieve a small, plastic bottle of mineral water. She handed this to Ellie, then opened the glove compartment and took out a small thermos for herself. She unscrewed it and took a swig, swallowing several times.

"Ahhh..." she said at last, lowering the thermos. She glanced at Ellie, who was watching her curiously, and said with an apologetic smile, "Sorry I can't offer you any. It's a personal health drink—"

"Oh no, that's OK," said Ellie quickly. "I just wondered what it was. Is it an American thing to drink health drinks in the mornings?"

Nancy laughed. "Dunno. Maybe it's just me. There sure is a big market for supplements and stuff like that, though. Vitamin smoothies. Herbal tonics. Superfood tinctures. Big business, here in America." She raised the thermos. "Helps to wake me up and get the blood flowing, you know?" she said, leaning back and taking a deep breath, then exhaling gustily.

It was true that the color seemed to be coming back into Nancy's cheeks and her eyes seemed brighter. She replaced the thermos in the glove compartment, then pulled out a packet of mint gum and popped several pieces into her mouth.

"Want some?" she asked Ellie.

"Oh, no, thanks." Ellie glanced at the tube the other woman was holding out to her. "Is that some kind of special herbal gum too?"

Nancy laughed. "Nah. This is just regular gum. Although I'm sure there's special herbal gum too." She glanced at Ellie and asked, "What about Vitamin

C? You ever take anything like that?"

"No, not really," said Ellie, thinking the woman sounded like a health fanatic. "I might have a hot honey-and-lemon drink when I've got a cold but that's about it."

"Well, one thing you should have is water and lots of it," said Nancy, gesturing to the bottle in Ellie's hands. "It can get really hot and humid here in Florida and if you're not careful, you can get dehydrated easily."

"Thanks," said Ellie. Nancy might have been a bit obsessive about health supplements, but it was nice of her to be so caring.

And it was true that it was a lot hotter than Ellie had expected. You might read about a place being "hot" but it was totally different when you experienced it! It was a lot more humid too. Ellie looked up and caught her reflection in the rear-view mirror. Her normally curly hair looked frizzier than ever. She was grateful that Nancy had turned the air-conditioning on full-blast.

"Is it always this hot in November? Or is this some kind of freakishly hot weather?" Ellie asked.

Nancy burst out laughing. "This isn't hot! You should see what it's like in July. But to be fair, this is warmer than usual for November. We don't normally get temperatures in the seventies this early in the morning. Winters in the Tampa Bay area are always pretty mild, though—it's what everyone comes here for: the warm, sunny weather. Our peak tourist season is from January to March. The traffic can get pretty crazy down here around that time..."

Nancy trailed off as she navigated the car out of the airport and onto the highway. She seemed to be struggling to concentrate and the car swung wildly out of its lane several times. Finally, they settled down to a steady speed on the highway. Ellie relaxed in her seat and felt her previous fatigue returning. She had to stifle a yawn several times as they drove across the Howard Frankland Bridge spanning Old Tampa Bay.

Nancy glanced at her and said: "I probably should've asked if you wanted to get a cup of coffee at the airport before we left."

Ellie covered her mouth and gave an embarrassed laugh. "That's OK. This is just jet lag. I didn't get much sleep on the plane and my body still thinks it's in a totally different time zone."

"It's a killer if you can't get some caffeine in the mornings though. Especially if you have to be up early, like I had to today to meet this flight." Nancy shook her head. "I'm not one of those early birds that bounce out of bed, that's for sure!"

Ellie gave her an apologetic smile. "I'm sorry my flight arrived so early."

"Oh no, it's not your fault!" said Nancy quickly. "Didn't mean to complain. To be honest with you, I should be used to it, being the resort chauffeur and all. I always have to pick up guests at all sorts of ungodly hours."

"It must be really hard if you're not a morning person," said Ellie sympathetically.

Nancy shrugged. "Don't have much choice. I need the job. I've got a son to put through college. Anyway, I'm used to it. I've been working all my life—never had the luxury of being a stay-at-home-mom or anything like that. My husband left me when our son was just five. The jerk ran off with the girl at the local diner, can you believe it? So it's only been the two of us ever since. 'Course, it helps that Mike is such a good boy; he's always looking out for his mom. But it's been pretty tough. I've had to do all sorts of jobs to keep a roof over our heads."

Wow, thought Ellie as she made noises of sympathy. *It's true what they say about Americans: they really do tell you their whole life story as soon as you meet them!* Still, there was something really nice about the woman's open friendliness and chatty manner—Ellie decided that she preferred it to the cool reserve she usually encountered back in the U.K.

Nancy was still talking. She grinned at Ellie and said: "I'm not fussy. There's nothing I wouldn't do to look after my boy. I've done waitressing, telemarketing, bartending, fruit-picking... but this is probably the best gig I've had. Aside from the occasional early-morning airport pickups, it's pretty cushy. The guests usually just want to go into downtown St. Pete or to one of the attractions in Tampa Bay, or occasionally some family will hire me to drive them to Orlando. It's pretty well paid and there's not many other jobs where you can spend the days looking out on this view, huh?" she added, gesturing out the windshield.

"It's beautiful," Ellie agreed, looking at the lush green landscapes as they drove through the attractive neighborhoods of the Pinellas County peninsula. She noticed several ponds and waterways, and scanned them eagerly as they drove past.

"Is it true that there are alligators everywhere in Florida?" she asked.

Nancy chuckled. "Well, maybe not *everywhere*, but there sure are a lot of them. If there's a pond or a lake somewhere, there's probably a gator nearby."

"Really?" said Ellie, wide-eyed. "But... are they dangerous?"

"I wouldn't get up close and personal with one, if that's what you're asking! But they won't bother you most of the time. Generally, gators are pretty shy of humans and keep away from us. They only really become a problem if they get used to being fed by humans. 'Course, if I had a young child or a little dog, I'd be super careful. Especially during mating season, when the males are migrating and moving around a lot more. But as long as you keep a safe distance, you should be OK." Nancy grinned at Ellie. "So... first time to Florida, huh?"

"First time in the United States," said Ellie with a big smile. She could see that Nancy was curious about her and after the other woman's chatty revelations about her personal life, Ellie felt obliged to reciprocate with a bit of personal information too. "I've been dreaming about having a warm beach holiday, especially as it was so cold and dreary in London, so it was like a miracle when I got the letter from my aunt, inviting me to join her here. She even sent me a ticket!"

"Wow," said Nancy. "Pretty sweet, huh? So your aunt's here already?"

Ellie nodded. "Aunt Olive's an author. She's attending the writers' conference at the resort—"

"Oh yeah, the delegates have been arriving the last couple of days. I picked up a few myself from the airport. I think the events kicked off last night, didn't they? I saw a sign for drinks in the lobby..."

She trailed off again to focus on the steering wheel and Ellie was glad. She was finding Nancy's driving a bit scary. They were traveling down a wide boulevard now, but the car seemed to be going too fast, even for the wide lanes, and they kept veering dangerously close to other vehicles.

Nancy saw Ellie clutching the door handle and she gave a rueful smile. "Sorry. Floridians tend to drive a little fast."

And a bit wildly too, thought Ellie as the car swerved suddenly, almost hitting the car in the next lane. The other driver yelled expletives out the window, but Nancy ignored him, accelerating even faster so that they pulled away.

Ellie was hugely relieved when they pulled off the boulevard into the driveway of a long, sweeping building. Manicured lawns and lush plantings lined the sides of the driveway, which ended at the front of two large white colonial doors—the main entrance of the resort.

The car lurched around the curve of the driveway a bit too fast, swerving close to the curb and narrowly missing one of the brass posts set on either side of the red carpet leading to the front door. Nancy jammed her foot on the brake and the car jerked to a stop just in time as Ellie let out a breath of relief.

"Here we are!" said Nancy, in a bright voice. "Welcome to the Sunset Palms Beach Resort!"

CHAPTER FOUR

Ten minutes later, Ellie joined the line of guests in front of the reception counter. She scanned her surroundings as she waited to be checked in, admiring the spacious lobby. Kids were gathered in front of an enormous aquarium dominating one wall of the area, pointing at the multi-colored fish. There were oversized pots containing miniature palm trees dotted between the couches and side tables displaying hurricane lamps and glass jars filled with sand, seashells, and driftwood.

Seashells seemed to be everywhere, even dangling from the chandeliers on the ceiling, and there seemed to be a "tropical birds" theme too: paintings on the walls showed off tropical birds like toucans, parrots, and flamingos, and there was even a scarlet macaw sculpture on a stand in the corner which looked so life-like that Ellie almost thought the bird was real. She couldn't wait to explore the resort once she had checked in and she was glad the line moved quickly. She was soon being served by a cheerful girl behind the reception desk.

"Oh yes, your aunt told us that you were coming, although she wasn't sure what date," said the girl.

"I didn't tell her on purpose," said Ellie with a mischievous smile. "Aunt Olive probably thinks I'm arriving next week so I thought I'd surprise her by turning up earlier than expected."

"It sounds like she'll have a wonderful surprise! Well, she's in the Beach Villas Wing: Number 12. That's one of our nicest suites, right by the pool deck and with a view of the beach." The girl handed Ellie a map of the resort and pointed out an area by the pool. Then she held out a color-coded plastic bracelet for Ellie to put on. "You need to wear this while you're in the resort—it identifies you as being on the full package, so you can get access to all the amenities and facilities. It includes breakfast, but your aunt also left a note to say that you should charge everything back to the room, so you don't have to worry about paying for any meals while you're at the resort."

"Wow!" said Ellie, not expecting that. "Aunt Olive is amazing!"

"If you wait a minute, I'll call one of the bellmen to help you with your luggage—"

"Oh, no, that's OK. I only have a small case

anyway. I can manage by myself," Ellie assured her.

She took the room card key and headed off, following the instructions on the map. She found the villa easily and knocked excitedly, imagining Aunt Olive's face when she opened the door. There was no reply. Ellie knocked again. Still nothing. After knocking a few more times, Ellie decided that her aunt must be out in the resort somewhere. Maybe she was taking an early morning walk on the beach?

I'll dump my things and go look for her, Ellie thought. Using the card key that the girl at the reception had given her, Ellie unlocked the door and stepped inside the villa. It was a luxuriously furnished suite, with wicker furniture and upholstery in soft beige and blue, like the colors of sand and sea. The seashell theme from the lobby continued here, with a large conch on display in the cabinet beside the TV and smaller shells decorating the light fittings.

Ellie walked through the suite, calling: "Aunt Olive? Hello, is anyone here?"

Silence met her as she passed through the open-plan living room and attached kitchenette to the two bedrooms, each with an en suite. The larger was obviously her aunt's, with various accessories and shoes strewn around the room, and clothes hanging in the wardrobe. The bed, though, was neatly made, the sides firmly tucked in, which made Ellie pause in confusion.

It looked like no one had slept here overnight, and

yet surely that couldn't be true? Where else could her aunt have slept? Maybe the maid had come in early and made up the room already? Ellie was doubtful. It was still very early and Housekeeping didn't usually clean guest rooms until much later in the morning.

It was strange, too, that her aunt would be out so early. Like Nancy, Aunt Olive was not an early bird. Ellie could remember her aunt often saying there should be a law passed that nothing should be open and no business conducted before ten o'clock and a decent cup of tea. *Still, maybe people behave differently on vacation*, she told herself. Or perhaps there was an early-morning lecture or workshop at the writers' conference which her aunt was attending.

She moved on to the other bedroom where she found a note on the bed addressed to her, plus a beach tote. The note was from her aunt and said:

Welcome to Florida! A couple of things to help you get settled in and ready for that first walk on the beach!
Love, Aunt O
xxx

Ellie smiled as she looked in the tote and found a sunhat and a pair of flip-flops. *Aunt Olive always thinks of everything!* She couldn't wait to put the flip-flops on and head down to the beach. But first, she needed to unpack. She went back out to fetch her case, which she had left in the hallway outside the door of the suite.

Just as she bent to pick up her case, something pale, brown, and scaly slithered out from beneath it. Ellie jerked back and screamed, dropping the case. A young woman in a Housekeeping uniform rushed out of a nearby room and hurried over to Ellie.

"What is it, ma'am? Are you all right?" she asked.

Ellie sagged against the wall. "Yes... I think... I think I saw a snake!"

"A snake?" said the maid doubtfully. "I've never seen one near the resort buildings. Are you sure it was a snake?"

Ellie indicated her case. "Yes! I'm sure I saw something slithering out from beneath my case when I tried to pick it up... Look! It's still there! Next to the left wheel!" She pointed frantically as she saw the reptile poke its head out again.

The maid bent to look, then burst out laughing. "That's no snake, ma'am," she said. "That's a skink."

"A skink? What's that?"

"It's a kind of lizard. You see lots of them around Florida. They've got tiny legs, see?" She pounced on the creature and picked it up, holding it out to Ellie, who shrank away in disgust. Then curiosity got the better of her and she leaned tentatively forward to look. She saw that the woman was right: the little reptile did have tiny rudimentary legs jutting out from its long, slinky body.

"It doesn't bite. It can't hurt you," said the maid, putting the skink back down again and dusting her hands off.

"Well, I wouldn't want to find that in my bed," said Ellie, making a face. Mentioning beds made her think of her aunt and she asked the maid: "By the way, do you service the rooms along this corridor?"

"Yes, ma'am," said the woman.

"Did you come in early this morning to make up the beds in this room?" Ellie pointed to her aunt's suite.

The maid shook her head. "No, I haven't been in there since I cleaned the room yesterday morning."

"And nobody else would go in? Like another maid?"

The woman shook her head again.

"Oh. Well, thanks." Ellie started to turn away but the maid spoke up:

"That's no problem, ma'am. My name is Maria. I look after your suite, so if you need anything, just let me know. Would you like me to help you with your luggage?" She lifted the case before Ellie could answer and carried it into the room, placing it in the second bedroom. Then she checked the bathrooms and gave the tables a cursory wipe. When she'd finished, she paused by the front door.

"Oh... erm, thanks for your help," said Ellie awkwardly.

Then she realized belatedly why the maid was waiting with such a meaningful look. Hastily, she dug into her pockets for some change. She wondered frantically how much she should give. She'd read that tipping was important in America and she didn't want to offend the maid with the wrong amount.

"Erm... here you are," she said, giving the woman some change and breathing an internal sigh of relief as she saw the woman's face light up with surprised pleasure.

"Thanks a lot! You have a nice day, ma'am," said Maria, leaving and shutting the door behind her.

Glad to be alone at last, Ellie wandered into the bedroom and sank down on the bed. It was soft and comfortable, and she flopped backwards onto her back, staring up at the ceiling. The excitement of arriving at Tampa Airport, followed by seeing the resort, had carried her along on a wave of adrenalin, but now that was fading and she was exhausted. She'd hardly had any sleep in the last twenty-four hours and it was beginning to catch up with her.

There was a soft breeze coming in through the open window, stirring the curtains and bringing with it the salty smell of the sea. In the distance, Ellie could hear children shouting and the sound of water splashing, mingled with the faint cry of seagulls.

I should really have a wash and unpack, then go look for Aunt Olive, she thought drowsily, stifling a yawn. But the bed felt so soft and comfortable that she just couldn't force herself to get up. Instead, she stretched out even more comfortably and, before she realized it, Ellie was fast asleep.

CHAPTER FIVE

When Ellie woke up at last, the room was dark and a faint glow could be seen through the curtains. She sat up in bed and looked at her watch in dismay. It was nearly seven o'clock! She had slept most of the day away!

Springing up, she went into the bathroom and splashed some cold water on her face. Then she went to check her aunt's room, followed by the rest of the suite. Everything looked exactly the same as when she had arrived several hours earlier. It was obvious that Aunt Olive hadn't come back. Suddenly, Ellie thought of her cellphone and clapped a hand to her forehead. *Duh!* Why hadn't she thought of it before? She must have been more tired than she realized that morning.

Hurriedly, she dug her phone out of her bag and

dialed her aunt's number. To her surprise, she heard a ringing from her aunt's bedroom and, when she traced the source of the sound, she found an expensive-looking rose-pink iPhone tucked amongst the cosmetics in the en suite. Aunt Olive had obviously left her phone in her bathroom.

Ellie felt a prickle of worry, then told herself not to be silly. After all, her aunt came from an older generation and she might not be glued to her cellphone like young people were. In fact, Ellie recalled that her own parents often seemed to leave their phones at home or forgotten in the glove compartment of their car. It was really frustrating when she was trying to get hold of them. Aunt Olive was probably similar.

Besides, what could have happened to her aunt in the middle of a busy resort? There had to be a logical reason for Aunt Olive's absence and she would probably turn up soon. In the meantime, all Ellie wanted to do was have a hot shower and change into fresh clothes. She had fallen asleep without even washing away the grime of her journey and now she felt disgusting.

An hour later, feeling refreshed after a long, luxurious shower and a thorough wash of her hair, Ellie let herself out of the room and headed toward the main resort building, where the lobby was situated. As she entered through the rear double doors, she was surprised to hear a loud buzz of laughter and conversation, and a minute later, as she rounded a pillar, she saw a large crowd of people milling around the lobby seating area. It seemed to be mostly composed of middle-aged women, and as Ellie got closer, she saw a sign beside one of the potted palms which read: "Forever Fiction Writers Conference—Welcome Drinks & Appetizers."

Perhaps Aunt Olive will be here? thought Ellie suddenly. She scanned the crowd, trying to peer over the heads and see if she recognized any of the faces. It was hard to see, so she moved around the edge of the crowd until she was standing next to the life-sized sculpture of the scarlet macaw. She was just standing up on tiptoe to try and see better when she was startled by a loud squawk next to her, and she reeled back in shock as she realized that the red parrot wasn't a life-sized sculpture... it was a living bird!

"*SQUAWK!*"

Ellie stared at the bird. "Erm... hello?"

The parrot flapped its wings excitedly and shouted: "*PEEKABOO!*"

By now, several people in the crowd were beginning to look her way. Ellie tried to shush the parrot, but it only resulted in the bird making shushing noises back at her.

"Shush! Be quiet!" Ellie pleaded.

"*BE QUIET!*" yelled the macaw.

More and more people were beginning to stare. Ellie felt her face going red with embarrassment. Across the lobby, a girl came out from behind the reception counter and hurried over. Ellie saw that it was the girl who had checked her in earlier.

"I'm so sorry, ma'am, is the parrot bothering you?" she asked.

"Uh... well, not really, except that it's making a lot of noise." Ellie glanced around, embarrassed at having caused a commotion.

The girl grinned. "Yeah, he can be super noisy. Most guests who know him are used to it though. He's the resort parrot."

Ellie gaped at her. "The resort parrot? You mean... he lives here?"

"Yup. We're a privately owned resort and the owner loves animals. So we've got a few unique features on the property—such as a resident parrot." The girl giggled. "We have a resident cat too." She glanced around the lobby. "She's not around at the moment but I'm sure you'll see her soon."

"Don't tell me you have a resident alligator as well," said Ellie with a dark look.

The girl laughed. "No, at least not yet. But you never know. Gators move around and we have a few ponds, so... you might get lucky and see one!"

"Oh my God, don't joke about it," Ellie pleaded. She turned back toward the macaw, who was tilting its head and eying her curiously. "Hello...?"

"*PEEKABOO!*" said the parrot.

"One of the guests must have taught him that," said the girl. "Hemingway's very good at repeating anything you say."

"His name is Hemingway?" said Ellie with a laugh. "How apt for a parrot in Florida." She leaned toward the macaw and said, "Hello, Hemingway. Nice to meet you."

"*NICE TO MEET YOU!*" The parrot made a kissing sound, then croaked, "*KISSY KISSY!*"

Ellie laughed. She was beginning to like this bird. "He's quite a character, isn't he?"

"Oh, yeah! Hemingway can be a real handful," said the girl with a rueful smile. "He's super inquisitive and he's always getting into things he shouldn't. But most guests find him really entertaining." She glanced back toward the reception counter. "Well, if you're all right, ma'am, I'm going to head back to the desk."

"Oh, sure. But please, do call me Ellie. Back in England, we only call the Queen 'ma'am!'"

"No way! Really? But what do you call a customer to be polite?"

Ellie thought for a minute. "In the posh places, they use 'madam' rather than 'ma'am.' But please— do call me by my first name."

"OK... Ellie," said the girl with a wink, then returned to her post.

Ellie turned back and stared at the parrot in fascination. Hemingway had the most beautiful plumage, with bright red feathers all over his body, and electric blue and yellow feathers on his wingtips.

A soft voice spoke up next to her. "He's really amazing, isn't he?"

Ellie turned to see a young woman standing next to her, looking at her shyly.

"Yes," said Ellie, giving the woman a friendly smile. "He nearly scared me to death, actually. I thought he was a sculpture or something when I arrived earlier today—"

"Oh my goodness, so did I!" cried the other young woman, laughing. "I nearly fell over when he moved and started talking!" She smiled at Ellie. She was slightly plump, with mousy brown hair and a sweet-natured expression. She was wearing a simple cotton blouse and pants, in neutral colors, and her face was bare of make-up. The only thing which stood out was a pair of brightly colored shell earrings which dangled from her earlobes. "My name's Ann. Ann Crosby. Are you a new member? I don't think I've seen you before. Although I don't know all the writers, of course—"

"Oh, no, no, no, I'm not a writer at all!" said Ellie with a laugh. "Sorry, I probably shouldn't be here, crashing your drinks party, but I was looking for my aunt. *She's* a writer. Her name's Olive Goldberg. She's a mystery author—"

"Oh my goodness! Yes, I know Olive. She's super nice! I'd actually been writing to her; I emailed her last year, asking her advice about a book, and I met her in person last night. So you're her niece?"

Ellie nodded. "Yes, Aunt Olive is my father's older sister. She invited me to come and stay with her at the resort. I just arrived this morning." She paused, then added, "Erm... I don't suppose you've seen my aunt anywhere?"

"No, not today, at least."

"But you say you saw her last night?"

Ann nodded. "Yes, at our welcome party. Well, actually, tonight is the official party, but we had some pre-conference drinks last night for all the people who arrived early. A lot of us were here already, even some big names like Lilian Fox—"

"Lillian Fox?" said Ellie, furrowing her brow at the unfamiliar name.

Ann's eyes widened. "Don't you know Lilian? She's like the bestselling romance author in the country. They say she sold a million books last year!"

Ann turned to point through the crowd at a tall woman who was wearing a sequined kaftan top paired with white slacks. Her big, bouffant hair was teased off her face and she wore bright red lipstick. She wasn't exactly beautiful, but her confidence a'

'nd glamorous appearance made her striking to look at.

"That's Lillian Fox," said Ann with awe in her voice, adding wistfully, "I wish I could write like her!"

"Do you write romance as well?" asked Ellie.

"Yes, sort of. Well, I suppose what I write is really more 'romantic suspense'—that's when you have romance with some mystery in it too. It's why I really enjoyed chatting with your aunt last night. She gave me so many good tips for the mystery side of the plot."

"Who's that woman?" asked Ellie, indicating the large woman standing next to Lillian Fox. She was wearing red lipstick too, although it clashed badly with her brightly colored, floral blouse, and did nothing for her looks. She was watching Lillian Fox with a sour look on her face. Every so often, she kept trying to interrupt Lillian, talking over her in a loud, brassy voice.

"That's Cheryl Jackson. She's the president of the NRWS—the National Romance Writers' Society. Or at least, she was. She's stepping down this month and Lillian is taking over," said Ann.

"Is that why she looks so resentful?" asked Ellie, smirking.

Ann grinned. "Yeah, partly. But also because Lillian's sort of taken her crown."

"What d'you mean?"

"Well, Cheryl always saw herself as Queen Bee, you know. She's awfully bossy and she always thought she knew everything; she loved lecturing you on how to write and how to promote your books. But then Cheryl's publishers dropped her. They'd been renewing her book deals every year, for the last ten years, but this year, they didn't. They signed Lillian on instead. Cheryl was furious. And then to make things worse, Lillian won this year's NRWS prize for Best Romance Novel. Cheryl has won that every other year. I wasn't at the awards ceremony, but I heard that Cheryl looked like she wanted to scratch Lillian's eyes out!"

"Wow... I didn't realize there was so much drama in the writing community," said Ellie, chuckling. "It sounds like it's going to be an interesting conference!"

"Will you join us for some of the social events?" asked Ann, giving Ellie a shy smile. "It'll be really nice to have you. I'm sure it'll be fine, as long as you pay for your own drinks and food and stuff. Some of the other writers have brought their partners along."

"What about you?" asked Ellie.

Ann blushed. "Oh no. I've come alone. I only—"

"*SQUAWK!*"

They both turned in surprise to look at Hemingway. The parrot, annoyed at being ignored, was bobbing up and down on his stand and flapping his wings. Suddenly, he gave a screech and took off from his perch. He swooped toward Ann, landing on her shoulder.

"Oh!" cried Ann, staggering back in surprise.

The macaw reached down and nibbled at her dangling shell earring, then gripped it firmly in his beak and tugged hard.

Ann gasped. "Ow! Let go! Let go!"

CHAPTER SIX

Ellie stared in horror, then she looked quickly around. She grabbed a glass of water from a nearby tray and threw it on the bird. The parrot screeched angrily, shaking the water droplets off his wings, then he took off, flapping away across the lobby. Ann staggered back, clutching her ear.

"Are you all right?" asked Ellie. "Did he hurt you?"

"Yes... I mean, no," said Ann, panting. She groped at her earlobe, then said ruefully, "Hemingway stole my earring!"

Ellie looked across the lobby to where the parrot was now perched on one of the oversized pots. He was holding the earring in one claw and chewing on it enthusiastically, bending and cracking the metal loop with his strong beak.

"Oh no, he's destroying it!" said Ellie.

"It's OK," said Ann, waving a hand. "It didn't cost much anyway. I got it from the gift shop yesterday. I suppose I could always go back and get a replacement."

"The resort should give you one for free, if you tell them what happened," said Ellie. "You shouldn't have to pay for it yourself, since it was their parrot who destroyed it."

Ann looked uncertain. "Yes, I suppose you're right. I just don't like to make a fuss..." She brightened as she saw a group of women coming toward them. "Anyway, never mind that now. Let me introduce you to some of the other writers."

Ellie spent the rest of the evening having an enjoyable time chatting with her new friends. She found the writers to be a friendly bunch and it was fascinating listening to them talk about their books and their writing process. Before she realized it, it was close to midnight. Even though she'd slept all day, she still felt very tired. So she decided to call it a night and, after bidding the others goodnight, she headed back to the Beach Villas Wing.

There was a figure walking ahead of her and as Ellie caught the sparkle of sequins on the kaftan the woman wore, she realized that it was Lillian Fox. They were walking in the same direction, but Ellie hesitated to call out. She had been briefly introduced to the bestselling romance author during the evening, but she had found Lillian to be cold and arrogant. Once Lillian had figured out that Ellie wasn't an editor, bookseller, or fellow author she could impress, she had lost all interest and completely ignored Ellie. Now she glanced at Ellie as she took out her key card, but she didn't acknowledge her with a polite "Good night" or anything similar. Instead, she opened the villa suite next door and disappeared inside without a backward glance.

Ellie unlocked her own door and stepped inside, looking eagerly around in the vain hope that her aunt might be there already, perhaps sitting on the couch and having a cup of tea. But the suite was empty. Ellie frowned. Where *was* Aunt Olive? She hadn't been at the welcome party either—Ellie had kept looking for her. It didn't make sense that her aunt would come to the resort for the writer's conference and then not attend the events. Ellie wondered briefly if she should go to the reception and report her aunt's absence, but it was late, past midnight, and there would probably only be a skeleton staff. Besides, what would they do? Her aunt was an adult. She had been seen at the pre-conference drinks the night before, so it wasn't as if she had been missing for days. The resort was hardly going to call the police because one of their guests wasn't in her room!

And Aunt Olive didn't even know I was arriving this weekend, Ellie reminded herself. It was her own fault for keeping things a surprise, so she could hardly complain now if her aunt wasn't here to greet her. *I'll go and speak to someone at the reception first thing in the morning*, Ellie decided. She was sure that nice girl she had met when she checked in would help. That way, she wouldn't feel like she was overreacting, but she also would feel less guilty and worried.

Ellie undressed and made herself a hot drink, then curled up on the couch and gazed out of the large, sliding glass doors, which looked onto a view of the private terrace and the pool area beyond. The villa suites were arranged in a row, with direct poolside access from their private terraces. Aunt Olive's villa was the first in the row, with Lillian Fox's villa the next one along. The private terraces of each villa were divided from each other by a bamboo privacy screen, and the ends of each terrace opened straight out onto the pool area, so that each villa's occupants could sunbathe in privacy on their own terrace, but also step off the terrace and be immediately on the pool deck.

From where Ellie was sitting, she could see straight out across the private terrace to the huge pool beyond. She could see the water shimmering with the underwater pool lights, and the dark shapes of the beach umbrellas and cabana roofs outlined against the night sky, as well as the tall palm trees swaying between them. It was a lovely, peaceful scene and Ellie leaned back against the soft couch cushions with a sigh. Her body was tired and she knew she should go to bed, but at the same time, her mind felt too wired and awake.

It must be the jet lag, she thought, glancing at her

watch and seeing that it was early morning in London. Her stomach seemed to be in the wrong time zone too. After not feeling hungry all night, she was now suddenly starving. She was about to get up and look in the kitchenette for a snack when a movement outside caught her eye.

Ellie paused and peered out into the darkness. *Was that...?* For a moment, she thought she saw a dark figure moving quickly across the pool area, toward her window. She blinked and looked again. No, it must have been her imagination. There was no one standing in her private terrace, no one coming up to the glass.

Ellie went to the kitchenette and rummaged through the cupboards, then returned to the couch with a fresh hot drink and a bag of chocolate chip cookies. As she settled back down on the cushions, she heard something that sounded faintly like voices, a laugh, an excited cry... She turned her head quizzically, then realized that it was coming from the adjoining villa. Lillian Fox's villa. She heard a high-pitched feminine giggle, followed by the low rumble of a man's voice. It sounded like Lillian had a male visitor. *Strange*, thought Ellie. She hadn't heard anyone in the corridor outside or the sound of Lillian opening her door to anyone. Even as she listened, a rhythmic thumping started coming through the walls. Suddenly realizing what the sounds could mean, Ellie blushed and hastily switched on the TV, turning up the volume to drown out any more sounds coming through the walls.

She had just finished watching an episode of a popular American sitcom when another movement outside the glass doors caught her attention again. She sprang up and hurried over to the glass, straining her eyes to see outside. She was sure she had seen a shadowy figure slip past and move across the pool deck, disappearing into the darkness. After a few more moments of staring out into the night, Ellie gave up. Feeling slightly annoyed, she drew the curtains so that she wouldn't be distracted by anything outside again, then she returned to the couch and watched another episode of the sitcom.

She found it hard to relax again, however. Somehow, she felt spooked and uneasy. So finally, she switched off the TV and prepared to go to bed. As she turned off the lights in the sitting room, she thought of the shadowy figure again and decided to make sure that the sliding glass doors leading out onto the terrace were locked. She went across and parted the curtains, then fumbled with the handle of the doors. As she did so, she looked absently through the glass, out toward the pool again.

Then she froze. She blinked and rubbed her eyes, then looked again. No, this time it definitely wasn't her imagination. There was something floating in the pool.

Ellie slid the glass doors open and stepped outside. The night air was warm and humid. She padded barefoot across the private terrace and then across the deck to the edge of the swimming pool.

She caught her breath and her heart jumped in her chest as she realized what she was looking at: a body floating face down in the pool. The underwater lights caught the sequins which sparkled on the kaftan that billowed out from the body.

It was Lillian Fox.

CHAPTER SEVEN

"Oh my God!" cried Ellie. "Lillian? Lillian, are you OK?"

The figure in the water was motionless.

Ellie ran around the side of the pool, panicking, wondering what to do. She knew she had to get the woman out of the water, but she didn't dare jump in the pool. She couldn't swim and she wasn't sure how deep the pool was. She was too scared to simply jump in the water—she could end up drowning herself. Turning, Ellie spotted an emergency phone nearby and ran over to grab it.

"Hello? Hello? Can you hear me? Yes! Yes, that's right—there's someone in the pool. She's floating in the water... She's not moving... I think she might have drowned!" she babbled. "I don't know how to swim. I can't get her out—you've got to get someone down here quickly!"

Several minutes later, Ellie stood at the edge of the pool and watched as several members of hotel staff helped to lift the dripping body out of the water. They lay the woman down by the edge of the pool and Ellie went over to look at her face: yes, it was Lillian Fox and she was very dead. She was clutching a cocktail umbrella in one hand and Ellie wondered if she had been holding a drink when she had been pushed into the pool. She looked around but couldn't see a cocktail glass by the side of the pool or in the water.

"Did you see what happened?" asked one of the hotel security guards.

Ellie shook her head numbly. "No, I just happened to look out of my windows and I saw something floating in the pool. I got curious so I went out to see what it was, and then I realized that it was a body."

"Did you recognize who it was immediately?"

"In a way. I guessed that it was Lillian Fox—she's one of the authors in the writer's conference. I met her earlier this evening and I recognized the kaftan she was wearing."

"Did you see her go out to the pool?"

"No, I didn't see her outside at all. I only saw her when we were walking back from the lobby together earlier. I mean, we weren't walking together. Lillian was walking ahead of me, but since our villas are next to each other, we were taking the same route."

"Did you see anyone else hanging around?"

Ellie thought of the shadowy figure that she thought she'd seen. Had she really seen it? Or had it been her imagination?

"Erm... I'm not sure. I thought I saw someone earlier, sort of lurking around the pool area."

"Man? Woman?"

Ellie shrugged helplessly. "I don't know. I couldn't tell."

"Are you *sure* you saw someone?"

"No... no, I'm not sure. It could also have been a trick of the light," Ellie admitted. She hesitated, then added, "I did hear some noises though."

"Noises?"

"Yeah, through the walls of the villa. Like voices and... and thumping."

"Thumping? You mean like in a fight?" the security guard asked quickly. "I checked the body and it looks like she'd been whacked on the head before she was pushed in the pool. This is looking like murder."

"Murder?" Ellie gaped at him.

He nodded grimly. "If Ms. Fox was unconscious, she would have drowned very quickly. Maybe what you heard were sounds of a struggle—somebody in her room attacking her?"

"No... erm... I don't think they were fighting," said Ellie, looking down and flushing with embarrassment. "Besides, that was like twenty minutes or half-an-hour before I saw the body. The person who attacked her could be someone else entirely."

Before the security guard could answer, one of the resort staff came over and said: "The cops are on their way."

The security guard nodded, then turned back to Ellie and said, "The police will want to question you, ma'am. Can I ask you to go back to your villa and wait there?"

Ellie nodded and obediently headed back toward the private terrace of her aunt's villa. She had to walk past Lillian's terrace on the way and she couldn't help pausing to look curiously around. It was like a mirror image of her aunt's terrace, with the same lounge and folded-up deckchairs, and same potted plant in the corner, just on the opposite side. She looked beyond the terrace to the glass sliding doors, which were partly open. She could see into Lillian's suite, which was also identical to her aunt's—except that it was a lot messier! There were clothes, hats, bags, and shoes thrown around the place. There were half-eaten bags of chips and cookie crumbs on the coffee table, as well as a couple of used wine glasses. But although it was messy, it didn't look as though there had been a struggle in the room: there was no overturned furniture, no broken glasses or ornaments, no signs of a fight. Whoever had attacked Lillian must have taken her by surprise.

Ellie turned to head back to her own villa, then paused as something shiny at the base of the bamboo screen caught her eye. She bent to pick it up and held it up to the light. It was a dangling earring in the shape of a shell and she realized why it seemed so familiar: it looked just like the one that Hemingway the parrot had ripped out of Ann's ear earlier that evening! It wasn't *that* specific earring though; Ellie could see that this one was still intact, whereas she remembered seeing Hemingway destroy the one that he had stolen. So this could have been the other one of the pair.

What did that mean? Had Ann been around here and dropped the earring by mistake? Was she the "shadowy figure" that Ellie had seen earlier? Ellie looked at the bamboo screen, with its rough fibers jutting out. If Ann had been skulking around and crouched down by the screen, her earring could easily have gotten snagged without her being aware of it. Then when she got up and moved away, the earring would have been left behind, and then maybe fallen down to the bottom of the screen. Or perhaps she dropped it on the ground closer to the sliding doors but had then kicked it here to the base of the bamboo screen without realizing it.

Ellie heard the sound of voices and the buzz of a walkie-talkie, and she looked up to see two men in uniform coming across the pool area toward her. The police were here. She hesitated for a second, then quickly slipped the earring into her pocket. She knew that it was evidence and she should give it to the police, but at the same time, she couldn't help remembering Ann's shy, sweet-natured face. She didn't want to get the other young woman in trouble. At the very least, she owed it to Ann to talk to her first and ask her about the earring before showing it to the police.

CHAPTER EIGHT

The next morning, Ellie was awakened by the sound of seagulls and she stared in confusion at the ceiling for a long moment before she remembered where she was.

Florida... Aunt Olive... Lillian Fox... The body in the pool!

Ellie sprang out of bed and hurried to her aunt's room, but it was empty, the bed still perfectly made. The wave of worry returned. This was the second night now that Aunt Olive hadn't slept in her bed. Where was she?

Ellie had tried to express her concerns to the police the night before, after they had finished questioning her about Lillian Fox. But the officers had been more interested in the murder than in a possible missing persons case.

"You said someone confirmed seeing your aunt at an event last night, right?" the detective had said. "So just because she wasn't in the room when you arrived this morning doesn't mean that she's gone missing."

"But her bed wasn't slept in," Ellie had protested. "It looks like Aunt Olive hadn't come back to the suite at all last night. And no one has seen her all day."

The detective shrugged. "The resort's a big place."

"Surely she would have been at the welcome party this evening? I mean, the reason she came to this resort was to attend the conference, so why would she miss the welcome party?"

The officer looked bored. "Maybe she decided to go somewhere else."

"What do you mean? Where else would she go?" asked Ellie, exasperated.

"Maybe she hooked up with a guy and he asked her out to dinner and she decided to ditch the writers' event."

Ellie wrinkled her nose. "My aunt's in her sixties; she's not a teenager! She's not going to just 'hook up' with some random guy she meets."

The officers shrugged again. "Maybe it was love at first sight."

Ellie had rolled her eyes. *Oh for goodness' sake!* Finally, the detective had agreed to look into things and left, leaving Ellie feeling like she was overreacting. Looking at the empty bed now, though, Ellie was sure she wasn't overreacting. Something about her aunt's disappearance just didn't feel right.

Sighing, she returned to her own room and walked over to the window. There was a great view toward the beach and the sea looked amazing: vivid aquamarine, with a line of white foam running along the shore. It was still really early but the sun was already strong and warm, and she could see the figures of several people walking and jogging on the beach. Suddenly, Ellie was seized by an impulse to join them. She would go for a brisk walk, she decided. The exercise would help her get over the jet lag. And then she'd come back, shower, dress, then go to the reception and speak to someone about her aunt. If the police weren't going to take things seriously, she would have to start doing some more active searching herself.

Ten minutes later, Ellie was striding across the beach, enjoying the feeling of the sand between her toes and the warm sun on her face. *If it wasn't for the worry about Aunt Olive's whereabouts and that grisly discovery in the pool last night, this would be the perfect vacation*, she thought, stretching her arms out wide and swinging them around. Then she began playing a game, running along the edge of the water, hopping and jumping to avoid stepping in the foam. She was enjoying herself so much and was so engrossed in the game that she didn't notice the large piece of shell protruding from the sand until it was too late.

"OWWW!" Ellie cried as she felt a piercing pain in

the sole of her left foot.

She clutched her foot and hobbled onto drier sand, then crouched down to examine the injury. There was a trail of blood across her sole and she was dismayed to see a deep gash.

"Are you all right?"

Ellie glanced up, shielding her eyes from the sun. There was a young man standing in front of her. He was at least six feet tall, with warm brown eyes and brown hair that was streaked golden by the sun. He was dressed in a T-shirt, shorts, and running shoes, and she could see sweat glistening on his tanned neck and muscular arms. As he came closer and bent down, she could also see that his handsome face was creased with concern.

"Are you hurt?" he asked. He had a pleasant baritone, with a light American accent.

"I cut my foot," Ellie said, grimacing. "I think I stepped on a broken shell."

"Let me see." The man crouched down next to her and took her foot in his strong hands. "Do you mind if I take a closer look?"

Ellie shook her head and leaned back to give him better access. She watched him examine her foot with great dexterity and authority.

"Have you examined a lot of feet?" she asked jokingly. "You look awfully experienced."

He smiled at her. "I should be. I'm a doctor."

"Oh! Really?" Ellie laughed. "I guess it's my lucky day, then." She peered at her foot. "Is it bad? Is it a deep cut?"

"Not too bad. It doesn't need stitches. But it will still need to be cleaned and dressed to prevent infection. Have you been fully vaccinated for tetanus? If not, you'd better get a booster, just in case. You need to watch out for vibrio infection too."

"What's that?" said Ellie, alarmed.

"It's an infection from *Vibrio vulnificus*, a kind of bacteria that's commonly found in shellfish. It can cause a fatal infection in some people. Don't worry," he added quickly, seeing Ellie's expression. "It's pretty rare if you're young and healthy. Your body's own immune system should take care of things. But that's why it's important to clean the wound thoroughly and to take antibiotics for a few days."

"We could scoop some seawater on it, can't we?" Ellie suggested. "Wouldn't the saltwater sterilize the wound?"

The handsome stranger grimaced. "Pure saltwater, yes, but seawater is full of other stuff, including vibrio bacteria. It's the worst thing you can do in this case! It's a very common myth; a lot of people are under the false impression that seawater is good for cuts and wounds, but it's totally wrong."

He rose and looked back up the beach, at the line of resorts facing the water. Each resort comprised a cluster of buildings, and they were all situated in a row, so that as you walked down the beach, you passed the section of sand assigned to each property in turn. Every resort had its own cabanas, lounges, and deckchairs arranged in rows facing the water, all color-coordinated for easy identification.

"I assume you're staying at one of the resorts?" the stranger asked Ellie. "If you tell me which one, I can help you back."

"Oh... erm, I'm staying at the Sunset Palms Beach Resort."

He turned back to her, his smile widening. "Really? What a coincidence! That's where I work."

"Work?" Ellie looked at him in puzzlement.

He nodded. "I'm the resort doctor." He held out a hand. "I'm Blake—Blake Thornton."

"I'm Ellie Bishop." Ellie looked at him curiously. "I've never heard of a resort doctor."

He laughed. "It's one of the unusual features of the Sunset Palms. The owner wanted a 'doc in residence'—to give the guests some peace of mind. Lots of luxury resorts have started to offer this kind of service. It's very popular with older guests who might have chronic conditions that need monitoring. But even families with young children really appreciate having someone onsite to treat minor bumps or injuries, without having to go to the ER. I do a shift at the local hospital too and I'm on call for emergencies at a few other resorts, but I live at the Sunset Palms full time."

He extended a hand. "Come on... I'll help you back."

"Thanks," said Ellie, struggling to get up.

She managed to stand but she didn't dare put her

cut foot down on the sand, in case she got more dirt into the wound. So instead, she tried to hop along. It was impossible, though, even with Blake's arm supporting her. The soft sand kept shifting under her feet, making it hard to get enough leverage to jump, and after a few feet, she had to stop, panting and exhausted. She looked in despair at the resort in the distance. It was so far! How was she going to manage it?

Blake watched her for a moment, then he reached out gently and picked her up, swinging her into his arms.

"Ohhh!" cried Ellie in surprise.

"Sorry—I hope you'll forgive the presumption," he said with a wry smile. "But it'll be quicker and easier this way."

Ellie wasn't sure what to say or think. She could feel a blush heating her cheeks and she had to look away as she said gruffly, "Yes, thanks."

Then, as he started striding across the sand, she found herself sliding her arms around his neck and leaning into his chest. It felt nicer than she wanted to admit and she didn't dare look up at Blake's face, staring instead at a spot on his shoulder. She had never had a man lift her in his arms like this.

Well, I suppose if you're going to get hurt on a beach, you could do worse than be rescued by a hunky doctor! thought Ellie with an inward smile

CHAPTER NINE

They caused quite a stir going up the beach, with families and couples and groups of tourists staring and pointing and smiling in a coy way. Ellie was glad when they finally arrived back at the resort and Blake took a roundabout route so that they wouldn't have to walk across the pool area, in full view of the other guests. Instead, he went down a side path that led around the back of the main resort building and arrived at a long building which seemed to house various offices.

"This is the resort clinic," Blake said as he shouldered his way through a door, walked through an empty waiting room, and lowered her gently onto the bed in the examination room.

He went across to the sink and carefully washed and scrubbed his hands, then opened a cupboard and took out several first-aid items. Ellie leaned back and gritted her teeth as he cleaned and disinfected the wound, then carefully applied some antibiotic ointment and a clean dressing.

"There. That should heal up in a few days. And here are some antibiotics—make sure you complete the full course. But if you get any vomiting, diarrhea, fever, or abdominal pain, then come back to see me immediately," Blake said.

He went back to the sink and washed his hands again, then he filled a glass from the water cooler and handed it to Ellie. "Here... have some water. You can get dehydrated very easily on the beach."

Ellie took the glass and drank deeply, while Blake filled another one for himself.

"Do you go jogging on the beach every morning?" Ellie asked.

"Yeah, most mornings. I like to get my exercise in before the day starts. Once the clinic opens, things can get chaotic. It's not usually too serious, but between the allergies and colds, cuts and bruises, it can be pretty busy." He glanced at his watch. "In fact, I wouldn't be surprised if patients start arriving soon..."

As if on cue, there was a knock on the door to the clinic and it swung open to reveal a middle-aged woman in a white shirt and black pants. It was Nancy, the resort chauffeur. She wasn't wearing her dark shades today and Ellie was surprised by how bloodshot her eyes looked.

"Oh! Sorry, Doc," she cried, seeing Ellie in the room. "I didn't mean to interrupt."

Ellie found herself flushing again as she realized how suggestive it might look, with her bare-legged on the bed, Blake in his running gear, and the two of them alone in the room. She was grateful when Blake spoke up in a calm voice:

"Oh, you're not interrupting. I met Ms. Bishop on the beach while I was out jogging. She'd hurt her foot so we came back to treat it. Anyway, we're done now. Is there anything I can help you with, Nancy?"

The woman rubbed her temple. "I was wondering if you've got any Tylenol, Doc?"

"Right here." Blake fished a packet out of a drawer and handed them to Nancy, adding sympathetically, "Are those headaches still bothering you? That's the third time this week you've come for Tylenol. You should get them checked out, you know." He glanced at his calendar, then added, "I'm free this afternoon. If you want to come by, I can do a quick examination and see if we need to send you to the hospital for some scans—"

"Oh no! No need for that," said Nancy. "I'm sure it's nothing. It'll go away with the pills."

"It would all be covered by your health insurance from the resort," Blake assured her. "You won't have to pay anything out of your own pocket."

"It's not that. It's just... I'm sure you're overreacting, Doc. It's no big deal. I... I just haven't been sleeping well. Nothing to worry about," said

Nancy quickly. "Gotta go now. Have a pick-up to make."

Blake looked at her in concern. "If you have a bad headache, maybe you shouldn't be driving. Do you feel any nausea? Or dizziness? How about any sensitivity to light?"

"No, no, I'm fine, Doc—honest!" said Nancy, backing out of the clinic. "It's just a headache and it'll be gone as soon as I take the pills. Thanks very much. See ya!"

The door swung shut. Blake stood staring at it and frowning.

"Do you think Nancy is ill?" asked Ellie. Although she'd only met the resort chauffeur the day before yesterday, she liked the woman and felt sorry for her. Nancy seemed to have a tough enough life already. The last thing she needed was some serious medical condition.

Blake shook his head and sighed. "I hope not. Nancy is a pretty sensible woman, so I hope she'll come see me if it's something serious. It's just that people can have such stupid ideas about pills!" he said in frustration. "I'm constantly getting people coming in here and saying, 'Hey Doc, can you give me a pill for this?' or 'Can you give me a pill for that?' They think they can just pop a pill for everything and fix it instantly. Well, what they're really fixing are the symptoms, and although it might make them feel better for a while, it won't make the problem go away. It'll just come back, and get worse and worse, unless they get to the root of the problem."

He sighed and ran a hand through his hair. "Like sleeping pills, for instance. A lot of people become completely reliant on them, instead of trying to use other methods to tackle their insomnia. I was talking to one of the writers at the conference, for example. She came in here yesterday afternoon and was asking about sleeping pills—for book research she said. She wanted to know if they could really knock you out and how quickly it would work. Apparently, she has a character in her book who takes them prophylactically to have a better night's rest! I tried to explain to her that the pills can be addictive and aren't something to be taken lightly. I thought it was important she portrayed this in her story, but she didn't seem very interested." Blake shook his head in exasperation. "You'd think someone who was the president of a romance writers' society with hundreds of members would be more socially responsible."

Ellie sat up straighter. "Wait... was her name Cheryl Jackson?"

Blake looked at her in surprise. "Yes. How did you know?"

"And she was asking about how to knock someone out with sleeping pills?"

"Well, not in so many words. She just asked how effective the pills were; whether they would really make you so unconscious that you would be unresponsive to stimuli, such as water in your face—

"

"What?" cried Ellie excitedly. "Oh my goodness, that could mean... Did she ask anything else?" She looked at Blake eagerly.

"No, not really. I told her that she really shouldn't resort to sleeping pills so quickly. If she's having trouble getting to sleep, she should try other things first, like decent exercise and a hot bath before bed. But she didn't seem very interested."

"Did Lillian Fox come to see you, by any chance?" asked Ellie.

Blake raised his eyebrows. "The murdered woman? No, she didn't. Why?"

"Oh. I just wondered..." Ellie slid off the examination bed and put her foot down experimentally on the floor. It wasn't so sore anymore. She found that she could hobble slowly as long as she didn't put too much weight on it.

"Make sure you keep the bandages dry," said Blake, putting a gentle hand under her elbow and guiding her to the small waiting room outside. "And if it gets red and swollen, or if you start feeling unwell in any way, then don't hesitate to come back and see me." He paused, then added with a smile, "In fact, don't hesitate to stop by, even if you're feeling fine."

Was he flirting with her? Ellie could feel her cheeks heating up again and she couldn't help a silly grin spreading across her face. She was about to reply when the clinic door burst open and a young woman came in, carrying a crying toddler.

"Doctor! Doctor, can you have a look at Hunter? He fell and skinned his knees, and he's got a bump on the head too."

"Sure. Come on in." Blake gestured toward the examination room, then gave Ellie an apologetic smile and followed them in.

CHAPTER TEN

As Ellie walked slowly from the clinic back to her villa, she couldn't stop thinking about what Blake had told her. Why had Cheryl Jackson been asking about sleeping pills? Why had she been so interested in knocking someone out? Was it really for book research? And that question about being responsive to water in the face… was that just a coincidence? Or could Cheryl have been involved in Lillian Fox's murder? Had she been looking for a way to knock Lillian out, so that her rival could be pushed into the pool and drown?

Ellie was so immersed in her thoughts that she barely noticed she was walking past the main resort pool until a child carrying an inflatable swim ring collided with her.

"Oops!" Ellie caught the little boy just in time

before he fell.

She gave him a smile as she set him upright, then watched as he trotted away, still clutching his swim ring. She realized suddenly that the pool area had been reopened. The police must have released the crime scene this morning. Looking around now—at the hordes of children squealing and splashing in the water, and their parents sunbathing on lounge chairs or sipping cocktails and munching on snacks delivered from the nearby *Hammerheads Bar and Grill*—it was hard to imagine that a dead body had been found here yesterday.

Then Ellie noticed a large woman stretched out on a lounge chair near her. It was Cheryl Jackson, wearing a lurid red swimsuit which didn't really flatter her skin tone or her figure. On an impulse, Ellie went over and sat down on the empty lounge next to her, saying in a gushing tone:

"Hi! You're Cheryl Jackson, aren't you? Oh my God, I love your books!"

The older woman sat up and took off her shades to eye Ellie haughtily. "Yes, I'm Cheryl. So you're a fan?"

Ellie nodded vigorously. "Oh yes, I've read all your books. Your writing is so amazing! I just love all your characters!"

"Really?" said Cheryl, a smile breaking out across her face and her manner becoming visibly warmer. As Ellie had guessed, Cheryl was like most authors in that she was easily flattered if you stroked her ego by praising her books.

"So which book is your favorite?" she asked Ellie.

"Oh... erm..." Ellie floundered. In actual fact, she had never picked up any of Cheryl Jackson's books and had zero idea what kind of characters and stories the woman wrote. "Oh, I love them all! It's so hard to pick a favorite," she said brightly. "Which one is *your* favorite?"

"Ah... Well, you know, it's impossible for an author to choose a favorite book. It would be like asking a mother to choose a favorite among her children!" Cheryl twittered. "Of course, there are some that I enjoyed writing more than others. And you always hate the book you're currently working on and think it's your worst book ever... until you finish it and then you look back and think: oh, maybe that wasn't so bad after all."

"It must be such hard work. I don't know how you do it!" said Ellie, giving the woman a look of exaggerated admiration. "And where'd you get all your ideas from?"

Cheryl laughed. "People are always asking that. Honey, the ideas are the easy part—anyone can have ideas! It's writing them down and turning them into a novel that's the difficult thing."

"I thought you just had to get an idea and write down what happens in the story," said Ellie, putting on a wide-eyed look. "I was talking to Lillian Fox the other day and she said that she just churns them out."

Cheryl scowled. "There's so much more to writing a story than just telling what happens, you know. There are the characters, the setting, the atmosphere... A lot of these new writers don't understand anything. They have no talent or experience or any real skill in telling a story."

"Do you think publishers don't really appreciate the work and effort involved?" asked Ellie innocently. "I mean, is that why they gave your book deal to Lillian?"

"They didn't give her *my* book deal!" snapped Cheryl Jackson. "Everyone is saying that, but it's not true! It just so happened that my new book proposal didn't fit with my publisher's schedule for this year. At the same time, they happened to offer Lillian a book deal. It was just a coincidence of timing. It doesn't mean that they took hers instead of mine!

"Of course, Lillian knows how to market herself— I'll give her that," added Cheryl grudgingly. "That's the real reason the publishers went for her, you know. Not because her books are anything much, but because she'll do anything on social media to get attention and promote her books. But I refuse to prostitute myself that way," she added, curling her lips in contempt.

"Really?" said Ellie innocently. "I guess the gossip got it all wrong."

"Gossip? What gossip?" said Cheryl, frowning.

"Oh... it was just some talk I heard last night at the party... some of the other authors talking..." Ellie deliberately trailed off.

"What were they saying about me?" demanded Cheryl.

"Oh, they were saying some really mean things," said Ellie, pretending to look embarrassed. "They were saying that you're crazy jealous of Lillian because she's taken your place as Queen Bee. Some of them were even worried that you're so threatened by her, you might do something you'd regret."

"That's garbage!" burst out Cheryl angrily. "Lillian hasn't taken my place at all! And what are they suggesting—that I might have murdered Lillian? Huh?" She leaned toward Ellie. "Who's saying all this?"

"Erm... I can't remember their names," said Ellie, not wanting to admit that she had made up everything to provoke the woman and get a response out of her.

"It's all a pack of lies!" snarled Cheryl. "Me jealous of Lillian? That's a joke! I've been doing this for years whereas she'd only been around the block for a year or two. Writing is a long game, I can tell you. And you know what they say: one swallow doesn't make a summer. Well, one bestselling novel doesn't make a career! So I have no reason to feel threatened by Lillian and I definitely had no reason to murder her!"

Cheryl Jackson turned her head to look across the pool area, then she pointed at a figure in the distance. "If they're looking for Lillian's murderer, that's the person they should be focusing on—not me!"

Ellie followed the direction of Cheryl's finger and found the other woman to be pointing at a handsome young man in the colored polo shirt and khaki uniform many of the resort staff wore. He looked Latino, with smoldering dark eyes and a dazzling smile, which he lavished on the female guests as he went around offering cocktails from a tray. They gave him coy looks and flirtatious smiles in return, and it was obvious that he was very popular amongst the women.

Ellie watched as he returned to the Tiki Bar, which had been set up in one corner of the pool deck, and began mixing more cocktails with expert skill. A few minutes later, he stepped out from behind the bar counter with a new tray of drinks and began walking around the cabanas and lounge chairs again.

"Who's that?" she asked Cheryl.

"That's Paolo," said Cheryl, leaning back with a smug look on her face. "He's the main waiter at the Tiki Bar and he's *very* popular with the ladies. Lillian was no exception. In fact, I think she was giving him some special one-on-one attention, if you know what I mean..."

Ellie pretended to look scandalized. "You mean they were having an affair?"

Cheryl gave a harsh laugh. "I wouldn't dignify what they were doing with the term 'affair.' Lillian had the morals of an alley cat. But then, I suppose if you sleep around, you'll have to take the consequences."

"Are you saying that you think Paolo had something to do with Lillian's murder?" asked Ellie.

Cheryl gave her a loaded look. "Everyone knows that murders are usually committed by someone the victim knew. And who knew Lillian better than someone she was sleeping with? Maybe they had a fight and things got a bit rough... Or maybe Lillian got jealous and started getting too demanding. I mean, Paolo is popular with a lot of the ladies here. Maybe Lillian wanted exclusive rights, and he wouldn't give them to her... Who knows? But if anyone was with Lillian late last night, I'll bet it was him."

At that moment, Paolo walked up to a couple sitting near them and handed them each a cocktail. Then he fished in his shirt breast pocket and took out two tiny paper umbrellas. He placed one on each drink with flourish.

Ellie caught her breath as she stared at the tiny pink umbrella sticking out of the piña colada on the table next to her. It looked identical to the one that Lillian Fox had been clutching in her hand when her dead body had been fished out of the pool!

What did that mean? Was Cheryl Jackson right? Ellie thought of the thumping and the embarrassing sounds she had heard through the wall. Had Paolo come to visit Lillian last night for some bedroom activity? Was he the dark figure that Ellie had seen slinking around the pool?

And was he the person who had knocked Lillian over the head, pushed her into the pool, and murdered her?

CHAPTER ELEVEN

When Ellie finally left Cheryl Jackson and returned to her villa, she found a police officer standing outside the door.

"Ms. Bishop? Detective Carson would like a word with you," he said.

"Oh. Of course," said Ellie, a bit surprised. The police had questioned her for a long time last night and she thought they'd covered everything.

She followed the officer as he led the way back to the lobby, and then through a door behind the reception counter. They walked down a long corridor which had several offices leading off from it and arrived at last at a small conference room where a middle-aged man with receding hair and a potbelly was waiting. Ellie recognized him as Detective Carson, who had questioned her last night.

"Thanks for coming, Ms. Bishop," he said briskly after inviting her to sit down. "I'd like to ask you some questions about your aunt."

"Oh, I'm so pleased! I was going to contact you about her actually," said Ellie quickly. "Aunt Olive still hasn't turned up and I'm getting really worried now. I think something bad may have happened to her! I know you thought I was overreacting last night but I'm glad you're taking my concerns seriously now!"

"I *always* took them seriously," said the detective. "That's why I want to ask you some more questions. For a start, what do you know about the relationship between your aunt and Lillian Fox?"

Ellie looked at him, confused. "What's that got to do with my aunt going missing?"

The detective ignored her words. "Did your aunt ever mention Lillian Fox when she spoke to you?"

"No, I'd never even heard of her before I arrived in Florida."

"What about the other writers? Did she talk about them?"

"Well, not specifically. She didn't really mention any names. She just told me about the writers' conference that was taking place at this resort."

"And you're sure she never mentioned Lillian Fox? Or any personal issues she might have had with another author?"

Ellie looked quizzically at the detective. "Yes, I'm sure. Look, what does any of this have to do with

Aunt Olive disappearing?"

Carson gave her a grim look. "We think your aunt's disappearance is linked to Lillian Fox's murder."

"You mean... she could have been a victim too?" asked Ellie. She gasped, putting a hand to her mouth. "Do you think the killer got rid of Aunt Olive first, so that she wouldn't be around to witness anything? I mean, they couldn't have known that I was coming to join my aunt. So they probably thought that by getting rid of Aunt Olive, the villa next door would be empty and the coast would be clear!"

"You think that's what happened?"

"Well, don't you think that it's odd Aunt Olive should disappear the day before Lillian Fox is murdered? Surely you can't deny that it's a strange coincidence?"

"I don't deny it. In fact, I don't think it's a coincidence at all. I think it was planned." Carson leaned forward and looked Ellie straight in the eye. "I think your aunt disappeared on purpose. I think she's responsible for Lillian Fox's death."

"What?" Ellie stared at the man incredulously. "You think Aunt Olive murdered Lillian Fox? Are you bonkers?"

The detective stiffened. "It's a reasonable assumption. Your aunt had the perfect opportunity. She knew Lillian's routines and habits, since she had a room next door—"

"Yes, but why on earth would Aunt Olive want to kill Lillian? She has no motive!"

"Not what I heard. Apparently, the two women were hostile toward each other. They were seen having a 'huge fight' on the night right before the murder."

"What? Aunt Olive and Lillian having a fight?"

Carson nodded. "Several witnesses saw your aunt arguing with Lilian Fox on the night before the murder, when the conference members got together for drinks. Lots of hostile shouting and name-calling. It got so bad, in fact, that the bartender had to come break it up. 'A real catfight'—that's how he described it. And it seems that your aunt made threats to Lillian Fox."

"Aunt Olive making threats? You've got to be joking!" scoffed Ellie.

"Witnesses clearly overheard your aunt say to Lillian: 'I'm going to put an end to your bullying once and for all!'—now doesn't that sound like a threat to you?"

"Aww, come on! That's hardly a death threat. You can't seriously believe that my aunt is a murderer just because she spoke out against a bully?"

"You said yourself that it's too much of a coincidence that your aunt disappeared right when Lillian Fox was murdered."

"So what are you suggesting? That she murdered Lillian and has... gone on the run?" asked Ellie sarcastically. "All her stuff is still at the villa. Even her purse with her wallet and credit cards and ID and things. Don't you think she would have taken some clothes and money if she was planning to make a getaway?"

"Not necessarily," said Carson. "She could have planned all this in advance and had a second set of ID and credit cards. After all, if she's going on the run, she wouldn't want to use the old ones. It'll be too easy to trace her that way."

Ellie started to argue again, then decided that it was a waste of time. The detective had obviously made up his mind about her aunt and wouldn't be willing to listen to her anyway. So she said nothing while he instructed her to remain at the resort, in case he wanted to speak to her again.

"Where else would I go?" Ellie muttered under her breath. "It's not as if it's a quick drive back to London."

Carson ignored her grumbling. "And if you do hear from your aunt—if she tries to contact you in any way—I want you to notify the police immediately," he said, giving Ellie a hard look. "Is that clear?"

***

After Ellie returned from the lobby, she finally managed to shower and wash off the sand and sweat from her walk on the beach that morning. Then, feeling clean and refreshed, she dressed in a T-shirt and shorts and set out to look for lunch. The resort had several dining options but Ellie decided to head back to the *Hammerheads Bar and Grill*. She'd liked the look of the menu when she was there for drinks with the writers' conference the night before, and she was curious to try some of the items for herself.

The restaurant had tall, bi-fold glass doors all along one wall, and these were all open now, so that the interior space flowed out onto the terrace overlooking the pool. Ellie chose one of the outdoor tables and sat down at a table shaded by a large umbrella. A middle-aged, African American man dressed in khakis and a polo shirt with the resort's palm tree logo came over and handed her the menu.

"What can I get you?" he asked with a smile.

"Erm..." Ellie examined the menu. There were so many delicious-sounding items that she didn't know what to choose. "Is there anything you'd recommend? Like a local specialty?"

"First time to Florida?"

Ellie nodded. "First time to the U.S."

"Is that right? Well, well... welcome to America! My name's Sol. I'm the head waiter here."

"I'm Ellie," she said, returning his smile.

"If this is your first visit to the Sunshine State, then you gotta try a Cuban sandwich," Sol declared. "It's a state icon."

"A sandwich from Cuba is an icon of Florida?" said Ellie in puzzlement.

Sol laughed. "It's not actually from Cuba—it was invented by the migrant workers here in the early

1900s and it's a mix of all their cultures: the Germans, the Italians, the Spanish, the Cubans..." He tapped the menu. "And we do the best Cuban sandwich in town—Tampa-Bay-style, of course."

"What do you mean, Tampa-Bay-style?"

He grinned. "Well, now, there're two ways to make a Cuban sandwich: the Miami way and the Tampa Bay way. They both got Spanish ham, roast pork, Swiss cheese, and German pickles and mustard on Cuban bread, but us folks in Tampa add a slice of Italian salami too." He made a gesture of kissing his fingers. "And that makes all the difference! It's usually served hot: grilled and pressed, but you can have it cold if you prefer."

"Sounds wonderful," said Ellie, her mouth watering already at the description. "I'll have a hot Cuban sandwich then!"

"And to drink? If you haven't tried our OJ yet, I recommend that. You'll never taste anything like the oranges in Florida!"

When the tall glass of orange juice was brought a few minutes later, it lived up to Sol's promise. It was cool and sweet, yet tangy and full of flavor. Ellie drained the entire glass, then set it back down and smacked her lips.

"Absolutely delicious!" she said. "I don't normally like orange juice much, but that was amazing."

Sol grinned, looking pleased, then a few minutes later, he brought her the Cuban sandwich. Ellie bit into it and savored the taste: the bread hot and crispy, the cheese melting slightly, and the ham and meat pressed together for each juicy mouthful. She demolished everything in a few minutes and when Sol came past again, his eyes widened.

"Man, that went down fast!" he said. "Looks like you enjoyed it, huh?"

"Oh, it was so yummy, I almost want to order another," said Ellie, laughing.

"Better save some space for dessert! How about some Key lime pie?"

"What's that?"

Sol gave an exaggerated look of horror. "You don't know what Key lime pie is? We gotta fix that right away! Wait here!"

He was back a few minutes later with a slice of pie on a plate. It had a thin crumb crust topped with a creamy yellow filling, finished off with fluffy whipped cream. Ellie took a forkful.

"Mmm... this is amazing," she said with her mouth full. "It's sort of tart and sweet at the same time, and the crust is so crisp and crumbly."

"Yup! Our Key lime pie is the best in town too," said Sol with a wink. "Well, now you can say you've tasted the state pie of Florida."

Ellie lingered for a while at the table after all the food had been cleared away, enjoying a cup of coffee while she watched children playing in the pool. With her belly full of food, she was beginning to feel drowsy. She hadn't slept very well during the night, and now she found that she was struggling to keep her eyes open. The jet lag was obviously still playing havoc with her body. Deciding not to fight it, Ellie paid her bill, leaving a generous tip for Sol, then found herself a free lounge chair at the poolside and stretched out.

She dozed for a few hours, awaking at last as the sun was beginning to slip down the horizon. She sat up and looked around. The pool deck was relatively deserted now. The sun had moved around, so that the main resort building cast a shadow, causing most of the pool to be shaded—which probably explained why many families seemed to have moved down to the beach.

Ellie idly watched some of the uniformed resort staff go around collecting empty cocktail glasses and used towels from the lounges, whilst others were busy re-plumping the cushions in the empty cabanas. Over by the Tiki Bar, she could see Paolo setting up a blackboard sign with the words "Happy Hour by the Pool" written in chalk. As she watched, he glanced down as his cellphone beeped suddenly with a text message. He took the phone out of his pocket, looked at the screen, and frowned as he read the message. Then he glanced up, looking furtively around, as if checking to see if anyone was watching him. The next moment, he ducked quickly behind the Tiki Bar and disappeared into the dense greenery behind the makeshift hut.

Ellie stared for a moment, then on an impulse, she sprang up and rushed after him. It was obvious from his actions and body language that Paolo hadn't wanted to be seen or followed. Why? Where was he going? Ellie ducked behind the Tiki Bar and found that there was a small trail leading deep into the dense landscaping surrounding the pool. She hesitated a second, then plunged down the path after Paolo.

CHAPTER TWELVE

Ellie walked quickly along the narrow trail, pushing back fronds and leaves, and trying not to think about the slithery reptiles or native creepy crawlies that might have been in the undergrowth around her. Instead, she kept her eyes on the figure in the distance ahead, moving swiftly through the dense plantings. Paolo was going so fast that it was obvious he was familiar with this trail and had used it many times. He paused once or twice to glance over his shoulder, and Ellie had to duck behind a large fern or a hibiscus bush to avoid being seen, but otherwise he didn't seem to realize that he was being followed.

They emerged at last in a place where the greenery surrounded a large paved area. Ellie realized that it was a small parking lot. It probably served the resort staff and any visiting suppliers, as she saw a large food van parked near the resort buildings on the other side. There were also two large dumpsters at the edge of the parking lot and Paolo headed for these. He stopped beside them and looked down at his phone again, shifting his weight nervously.

He's meeting someone, thought Ellie. She crept closer until she was several feet away from Paolo but still concealed in the dense greenery. She wondered who he was waiting for and, a moment later, her question was answered when a dark-haired young woman slipped out of a side door from one of the resort buildings and hurried over to the dumpsters. Ellie's eyes widened as she recognized the woman in the Housekeeping uniform. It was Maria, the maid she had met on the first day she arrived at the resort.

Maria threw her arms around Paolo's neck and tried to kiss him. He looked a bit annoyed and gave her a quick peck, then pushed her firmly away. She began talking to him in a rapid, passionate manner. From the scowl on Paolo's face and the irritable way he was gesticulating, though, it looked like they were having some kind of an argument, but they were too far away for Ellie to hear what they were saying clearly.

She bit her lip. She was afraid that if she moved any closer, they would see her. Then she brightened. She realized that the dense bushes and other greenery which surrounded the parking lot also curved around behind the dumpsters. If she could make her way to there, she would be right behind the couple and be able to eavesdrop on their conversation without being seen.

Staying in a crouched position, Ellie began moving through the undergrowth. Luckily, the plants were especially lush here, with large shrubs and creeping vines forming a dense green wall around the parking lot. As long as she kept low, they were unlikely to see her. Almost crawling on all fours, she made her way around to the patch of vegetation behind the dumpsters and slowly moved forward until she was at the edge of the greenery. Both Paolo and Maria were standing with their backs half-turned to her, but thankfully the wind was blowing in this direction and their voices drifted over clearly.

"...I know you were sleeping with her. Admit it!"

"So what if I was? I never said we were exclusive, did I?"

"How dare you! You told me it was only me. Me!" Maria clenched her hands into fists. "I will kill any woman who tries to take you away from me."

Paolo scowled at her. "You don't own me, Maria. We agreed we would have a good time together, but I'm a free man. If I want to go with another woman, that is my business—"

"But why her?" cried Maria. "She was old! Do you know how many anti-wrinkle creams she had in her bathroom?"

"So what? She was still a sexy woman. Older women are more fun in bed. They know what they want..."

"You disgust me!" said Maria, curling her lips back. "I cannot believe that I protected you when the police questioned me—"

"What did you tell them?" Paolo demanded. "Did you tell them that I was with Lillian last night?"

Maria crossed her arms. "No. But I still could tell them."

Paolo cursed in Spanish. "You would not dare do that!"

Maria looked at him insolently. "Oh yeah? It would be good payback for the way you treated me. Anyway, so what if they know? You were only sleeping with Lillian, you said. You didn't kill—" She broke off suddenly and looked at Paolo with a new expression. "Paolo, did you have something to do with her murder?" she asked in a hushed voice.

"No, of course not!" snapped Paolo. "I told you, I was only sleeping with her. Lillian was fine when I left her. But all the same, I was there last night—I visited her villa just before they found her body—and I don't want the police to know that. You know what people are like: the minute there is a Latino involved, everybody will jump on him as the criminal—*Shh!* What's that?"

He broke off and turned sharply to look in Ellie's direction. At the same time, Ellie heard a loud rustling in the undergrowth behind her. She jerked around and peered at the dense foliage. She saw branches moving, leaves swaying... something was moving through the greenery toward her.

Her heart began pounding in her chest as she peered into the dense green gloom. Wild thoughts entered her head. *What's making that rustling? Oh my God, what was it that Nancy had said about alligators? That they can migrate and travel over land, especially during the mating season, right? Is it mating season now? And that girl at the reception! She'd also mentioned that alligators move around. Didn't she say that they have ponds and canals in the resort grounds? Oh my God, is that an alligator moving through the undergrowth toward me?*

Ellie was about to scream and jump out from her hiding place, regardless of whether Paolo and Maria might see her, when the rustling stopped. She held her breath and waited but nothing happened. It was all still and silent around her. Behind her, she could hear Maria's voice asking plaintively:

"What is it, Paolo?"

"Shh!" he shushed her. His face was hard and suspicious as he peered at the greenery around them. "I heard rustling... I think someone's there..."

He came closer, stepping off the asphalt and taking a few steps into the vegetation behind the dumpsters. Ellie found her heart pounding for a different reason now. She tried to shrink down even lower in the undergrowth and wondered if her faded T-shirt would provide enough camouflage. She held her breath, watching through a gap in the leaves as Paolo came closer and closer...

Any minute now, he would see her. How was she going to explain what she was doing, skulking in the undergrowth and obviously eavesdropping on their conversation?

Suddenly there was a loud rustle next to her and a shape erupted from the bushes. Ellie clapped a hand over her mouth to muffle a scream just as Paolo jumped back with a cry of surprise.

"*MIAOW!*" said a black cat, strolling over to rub itself against Paolo's ankles.

Maria burst out laughing. "It is just the resort cat!" She clutched her middle and doubled over with laughter. "You should have seen your face, Paolo! You look like you'd seen the devil!"

Paolo cursed under his breath and made a kicking motion at the cat, who dodged his foot easily and gave him a dirty look.

"Filthy animal," muttered Paolo. "I hate cats. I don't know why the resort management keeps her around."

"Because the guests love her," said Maria, bending to stroke the cat. "You know Sunset Palms has a name for being a resort for animal-lovers. It is like that crazy parrot. He is terrible! But still, they let him fly everywhere." She straightened and looked at him. "Anyway, why are you so worried? What did you think was there?"

Paolo glanced at the greenery behind him again. "I thought maybe someone was there, listening to us."

Maria laughed again. "What is wrong with you, Paolo? Why are you so nervous? You said nobody else knew that you were with Lillian last night, except me." She narrowed her eyes at him. "Or are you not sure?"

"No, I'm sure," said Paolo. "I entered her villa from the terrace at the back and when I left, I made sure nobody saw me. There was no one around anyway. That part of the resort is really quiet at night. The only person I saw was one of the writers from the conference—the one with the stupid earrings. She dropped one by the pool earlier and I had to waste so much time helping her look for it. We searched everywhere for it: under the lounges, behind the cabanas... and in the end, she found it still stuck in her hair! Stupid woman."

"How do you know she didn't see you?"

"Because she was coming up the path toward the door of the villa and I went the other way." He gave Maria a contemptuous look. "I was more careful than *you*. If the police are looking for anyone to blame for this murder, they're more likely to nab *you*."

Maria stiffened. "What d'you mean?"

"I saw your note—the note you left Lillian. It was on her coffee table when I went in."

"I... I don't know what you are talking about," said Maria, licking her lips nervously.

"Ah, don't play games, Maria! I recognized your handwriting," said Paolo. "Anyway, I did you a favor: I took the note with me when I left. If I hadn't done that, the police would have been sure to find it and you would be in big trouble now!"

"I never left any note in Lillian's room!"

Paolo laughed sarcastically. "You think I'm a fool? You could have easily gotten into Lillian's room with the housekeeping master key; you knew her routine and when she was likely to be out... besides, the message was such a giveaway: '*Keep your hands off Paolo or you'll be sorry*'?"

He gave a harsh laugh as Maria flushed bright red. Then he turned serious. "How do I know that *you're* not involved with Lillian's murder? Maybe *you* went into her villa after I left and attacked her?"

"What? You're crazy!" cried Maria angrily. "I never went to her villa that night. I left the resort straight after I finished my shift."

"Really? Because I stopped by your place after I left Lillian." Paolo looked at her thoughtfully. "You weren't home, Maria. So where were you?"

"I... I couldn't sleep. I went for a walk," stammered Maria.

Paolo gave a disbelieving laugh. "At midnight? Good luck telling that to the police. I've still got your note, you know. It would be easy to give it to them..."

"No! You can't do that!" cried Maria.

Paolo smiled smugly. "Well, it looks like we both have things we don't want the police to know. So as long as you keep your mouth shut about me, I'll keep my mouth shut about you, understand?"

Maria nodded miserably. Paolo laughed again and

put an arm around her shoulders. "Hey! Don't look like that, *cariño*. We can still have fun together! C'mon, I've got some time before my evening shift starts..."

He led her away and their voices faded into the distance.

CHAPTER THIRTEEN

Ellie waited until Paolo and Maria were out of sight before slowly getting up from her crouched position in the undergrowth. She stretched stiffly, wincing as her muscles protested from having been in a cramped position for so long. The cat looked up from where she had been sitting, washing her ears, and came over to Ellie.

"*MIAOW!*" she said.

Ellie bent to stroke the cat's soft fur. "I suppose I should thank you! You might have scared me to death, but you also saved me back there. I thought Paolo was going to see me for sure! Hmm... I wonder what your name is?"

She crouched down and felt around the cat's neck. There was a collar, as she had expected, and her fingers found a tag dangling from it. She tilted her head to read the name engraved on the metal tag: "*Mojito.*"

Ellie laughed. Well, of course, if the resort had a parrot called Hemingway, they *had* to have a cat called Mojito.

"Hello, Mojito—pleased to make your acquaintance," said Ellie with a grin. "I'll remember to save you a little piece of ham the next time I have a Cuban sandwich, as a thank you."

Mojito gave a chirp of approval, then turned and began trotting back through the greenery. Ellie followed at a slower pace, letting the cat lead. Mojito seemed to know her way very well, weaving expertly through shortcuts in the undergrowth. In no time at all, they were back in the area near the main resort complex and the lobby. Ellie went to the reception and was pleased to find the familiar girl behind the counter. She thought back suddenly to when she had checked in... only two days ago? Ellie couldn't believe how much had happened in that time.

"Hi. My name's Ellie Bishop. I'm in Villa 12—"

"Yes, I remember you," said the girl with a smile. "It would be hard to forget Olive Goldberg's lucky niece!"

Ellie gave a sheepish laugh. "I actually wanted to ask you about my aunt. Did she leave any messages for me? Or have you heard from her in any way?"

"Hmm... I don't think so, but let me check," said the girl. She looked on the computer system, then checked some files and cabinets behind the counter.

"Nope, sorry. Nothing here." She looked back at Ellie, her eyes bright with curiosity. "The police have been asking about your aunt though. They questioned me this morning. They think she might be involved with the murder!"

"Oh no, I'm sure they're mistaken," said Ellie quickly. "Aunt Olive can't be involved—or if she is, then it's probably as a victim."

"A victim?" said the girl, her eyes round. "You mean she's been murdered too?"

"No! No, I didn't mean that," said Ellie, horrified. "I just meant..." She trailed off, not knowing what she had meant. She was worried about Aunt Olive, but she still didn't want to believe that something *really* bad had happened to her.

"Are you Olive Goldberg's niece?" came a new voice.

Ellie turned to see a man, who had been talking to one of the bellmen nearby, coming toward her. There was a camera slung over his shoulder and his eyes gleamed with interest.

"Uh... yes, I am," she said.

He thrust a hand out. "Ted Baxter. I'm a reporter with the *Tampa Daily News*," he said. "You know the police have your aunt down as one of the chief suspects?"

"That's ridiculous!" said Ellie. "Aunt Olive would never murder anyone!"

He sidled closer and said, his voice low, "Do you think she might have gone on the run?"

"What? That's a crazy suggestion! Aunt Olive wouldn't go on the run!" said Ellie indignantly.

"Well, why is she missing, then?"

"I don't know! There could be all sorts of reasons. Maybe… maybe she was kidnapped or something—"

"Kidnapped? You mean by the murderer? Have you got proof of that?" asked Baxter, busily scribbling away on a notepad.

"No, but it's a more likely explanation than my aunt being the murderer," Ellie shot back.

"The police don't seem to think so," said Baxter. "I spoke to Detective Carson this morning and he seemed convinced that your aunt is the most likely perp. After all, she and Lillian Fox had a feud going, didn't they?"

"A feud?" said Ellie, making a face. "That's a bit melodramatic, isn't it? They just had a small argument at a party the night before—"

"It was a lot more than that from what I've heard," said Baxter, waggling his eyebrows. "I've been speaking to the resort staff and they said things got really heated. Besides, it's not the first time the two women clashed. I asked around the writers' community and it seems like there's a lot of bad blood between your aunt and Lillian Fox. There have been scenes at past conferences… Your aunt is pretty outspoken, right?"

"Well… yes, she is," Ellie admitted.

"And it seems that your aunt is one of the few writers who's not afraid to stand up to Lillian Fox and criticize her. I heard that she accused Lillian of taking advantage of new authors. They were arguing the night before the murder. Several people overheard your aunt threaten Lillian and say that she was going to end the woman's bullying once and for all."

"Yes, the police told me that," said Ellie impatiently. "But like I told Detective Carson, it's crazy to think that just because my aunt stood up to a bully, it means that she then decided to murder her!"

"So you think the police are crazy?" asked Ted Baxter, busily writing in his pad again.

"No! That's not what I meant. Don't write that!" said Ellie, watching him uneasily. She was beginning to regret talking to him. She should have known that the media was likely to twist her words to make for a more sensational story. "Look... erm... I need to go..."

"Oh, our readers would love an exclusive interview!" Baxter said quickly. "It'll be a chance for you to tell your side of the story, especially if you think your aunt was unfairly treated by the police—"

"No, sorry... I need to go," said Ellie, backing away from him.

She hurried away from the reception counter and out the front entrance of the resort. Then she stopped as she realized that she should have gone out the doors at the back of the lobby, which led toward the pool area. She had been in such a rush to get away from the reporter that she had gone in the wrong direction. She turned and was about to head back into the lobby again when she saw Nancy come out of the front entrance straight after her.

"Ellie!" called Nancy, hurrying up to her. "I was standing by the reception and I overheard you talking with that reporter just now." She glanced over her shoulder to make sure that Ted Baxter hadn't followed them out, then added, "I might have some information about your aunt, but I didn't want to say it in front of that reporter guy."

"You have information about Aunt Olive?" asked Ellie excitedly.

"Well, it might be nothing, but I thought I should let you know, just in case. It was on the night before the murder. A bunch of writers were here in the lobby, checking in and stuff. I was hanging around as well, waiting to pick up a guest, and your aunt came up to me and started asking if I knew anybody in the local area who had a fast boat and could make a quick getaway if necessary."

Ellie stared at the other woman. "Really? Those were her exact words?"

"Yeah, pretty much. She wanted to know if it would be possible to get away via a boat off the beach and then go into hiding somewhere nearby."

"But... where would there be to hide?" asked Ellie in confusion. "I mean, if you go out from the beach here, you'd end up in the middle of the Gulf of Mexico, wouldn't you?"

"Well, you could go down the coast," said Nancy. "With a fast, powerful boat and maybe a quick stop to refuel, you could get down to the Florida Keys in a few hours."

"The Florida Keys?" said Ellie in surprise. "Can you get there easily from Tampa Bay?

"It wouldn't be a quick daytrip, but it's doable. It's about thirty hours by boat if you're just sailing, but it would be a lot faster in a boat with a motor. There's actually a ferry that goes from Fort Myers to Key West. It takes about three and a half hours, I think. But you could do the same in a private boat, if you're willing to pay the money." Nancy paused, then added, "There are tons of hiding places down in the Florida Keys."

"Oh." Ellie looked at the other woman uncertainly. "So did you recommend someone to my aunt?"

"Yeah, I told her about a guy I know who does independent charters. He's got a really powerful boat and no one knows the Florida coast better than him."

"Erm... have you told the police this?" asked Ellie.

Nancy shook her head. "No, not yet. Well, when they questioned me yesterday, they didn't mention your aunt. They just asked if I'd noticed anything odd about Lillian Fox, 'cos you know, I picked her up from the airport. I'd actually totally forgotten about your aunt asking me all that until I heard you asking about her at reception just now. And then when I overheard you talking with the reporter..."

She paused, then said, giving Ellie a sideways

H.Y. HANNA

look, "It's true that a boat would be a good getaway method. Especially if it was dark and after midnight—there would hardly be anyone around to see you. You could walk right down to the beach, wade out into the water, and then get into a boat that's waiting."

"But surely you don't believe any local boat operator would agree to pick someone up like that, without a proper explanation?" said Ellie. "And if they had been hired for something like that, wouldn't they have heard the news about the murder by now and come forward?"

Nancy shrugged. "Yeah, but—"

"Nancy! What's this I hear about you hitting the posts again?"

They turned to see a balding, middle-aged man coming out of the front entrance and hurrying toward them. It was the hotel manager and his face was set in an angry frown.

Nancy flushed. "I'm sorry, Mr. Anderson. It was an accident. I must have misjudged the distance when I pulled up in front."

"That's the second time this week! We're not paying you to put dents and scratches in the resort cars, you know. That vehicle's going to need a touch-up on the paintwork now."

"I'm sorry. It... it won't happen again," said Nancy.

"It better not! After all the guest complaints about your driving, this is the last straw. If this goes on, Nancy, we'll be reviewing your contract."

"No!" gasped Nancy, her face going white. "No, you can't do that, Mr. Anderson! You know I need this job. Please, everyone makes mistakes sometimes... I... I've just had a bad week. I've been suffering from a headache and... uh... but I promise there's nothing wrong with my driving!"

"Yes, Nancy picked me up from the airport and I had no issues," Ellie spoke up.

The hotel manager seemed to notice her for the first time. "Are you a guest at the Sunset Palms, ma'am?"

"Yes, I'm in the Beach Villas Wing," said Ellie.

"Ah!" His manner changed as he realized that she was staying in one of the most expensive suites. "Ah, I see. I'm sorry, I didn't mean to... I wouldn't have spoken if I'd realized..." He cleared his throat. "I'm glad you had a good trip, ma'am, and found the service acceptable."

"Yes, I... I thought Nancy was a great driver," Ellie said. She didn't know why she was lying for the woman; somehow, she felt sorry for Nancy and she didn't want the woman to lose her job. "In fact, she gave me a great welcome and made me feel comfortable immediately."

Mr. Anderson looked mollified. "Oh. Well, I'm glad to hear that," he said. He turned back to Nancy and added gruffly, "I certainly don't want to do anything rash. But I'll be keeping an eye on you!"

He stomped back into the lobby and the large double doors of the main entrance swung shut behind him. Nancy let out a breath of relief, then looked at Ellie gratefully.

"That was really nice of you. I don't know how to thank you—"

Ellie waved a hand, embarrassed. "It's OK. I hope you don't get in more trouble. But, Nancy, if you *do* keep getting those headaches, you really should listen to Dr. Thornton and get yourself checked out. You can't just keep relying on vitamins and supplements and things, you know. If you've got a medical problem, you really need to get it diagnosed properly and treated."

"Thanks, I appreciate your concern," said Nancy, looking defensive. "Don't worry about me. I'm fine. Like I told Mr. Anderson, I've just had a bad week. It's probably a virus or something. You know, working in a resort, you're always meeting different people and catching bugs off them. Anyway, thanks for your help." She glanced at her watch. "I'd better make tracks—I've got another job coming up. See you around!"

CHAPTER FOURTEEN

Ellie walked slowly back to her villa, thinking about what Nancy had told her. It did seem very suspicious that Aunt Olive should have been asking about ways to make a quick getaway from the resort. Why would she have wanted to know that? Why had she disappeared just before Lillian was killed? And most of all, where was she now?

There has to be a logical explanation, Ellie thought. No matter what the police said or how suspicious the circumstances looked, she just couldn't believe that her aunt was involved in Lillian Fox's murder!

She looked up and realized that she had been so deep in her thoughts, she hadn't noticed that she'd left the lobby via a different route. She was now walking down a covered colonnade which curved around the side of the lobby and eventually joined up with the courtyard behind the main resort building. There was a series of shops lining the colonnade, like a miniature shopping strip, including a hairdresser, a jeweler's, a small art gallery, a boutique selling designer shoes and handbags, and a large store selling resort-branded merchandise, postcards, souvenirs, beach clothing, hats, and other tourist paraphernalia.

Ellie paused outside the store as she recalled that she didn't have a swimsuit. She'd been planning to buy one when she arrived in Florida. She peered through the store windows and saw a rack of swimsuits and bikinis at the rear. She decided to go in and have a look; at least it would help take her mind off her worries about her aunt.

After a bit of browsing, Ellie found a pretty lemon-yellow bikini in her size and took it over to the counter to pay. The shop assistant was a friendly, middle-aged woman who gave Ellie a wide smile and said:

"Hi there! I'm Lynn. Have you just arrived? I don't think I've seen you before."

"Yes, I'm a new guest."

"Ooh, your accent sounds English. Where're you from, honey?"

"London."

"*Oooh!* London! Big Ben, Buckingham Palace, those funky red double-decker buses..."

"Oh, have you been?" asked Ellie with a smile.

"No, but it's on my bucket list. I'd *love* to visit! But *you're* here visiting *Florida*! So you'll want to send a postcard back to your family and friends in London, right?" said Lynn smoothly, turning around and reaching for a rack of postcards. She placed this in front of Ellie and added, "Two bucks each or five for seven-fifty."

"Oh... erm... OK, I'll take one to send to my parents," said Ellie.

"Just one? Come on! You must have friends you want to send a postcard to! Five for seven-fifty is a great deal."

"All right," said Ellie, chuckling as she caved in. "I'll take five."

"And how about something for yourself, honey?" said Lynn. "Suntan lotion? Beach hat? Sunglasses? Flip-flops?"

"No, I don't need anything, honestly. I just—" Ellie broke off as something beneath the glass top of the counter caught her eye. She bent to look more closely. There was a pair of shell-shaped earrings on display, together with several matching pendants, bracelets, and rings.

Lynn, seeing her interest, quickly reached under and pulled the earrings out. "Aren't they beautiful? This is the last pair I have in stock. Here..." she said, thrusting them at Ellie.

Ellie took the earrings and examined them closely. Yes, they looked just like the one she had picked up from the ground beside the bamboo screen on Lillian

Fox's private terrace. *And also like the ones that Ann was wearing on the night of the murder,* she thought.

"Honey, they'll look awesome on you!" Lynn gushed. "Perfect for any occasion, gives you a wonderful beachy vibe, and you know, seashells are always in fashion—"

"I don't suppose you know who bought the other pairs?" Ellie interrupted.

Lynn stopped, surprised. "We don't keep a record of names. I'd have to look at the receipts; if they paid by credit card there might be a name, but if they paid in cash... Anyway, I wouldn't be authorized to give out that kind of information." She looked at Ellie strangely. "Why are you asking?"

"Oh... erm... I was just curious. Uh... a friend of mine is one of the writers at the conference and she was raving about a pair of shell earrings that she'd bought. She said she got them from the gift shop—I just wondered if these were the ones she meant."

"I'm sure they are! They've been so popular. Beautiful but affordable. Even some of the resort staff have bought things from this line. And yeah, now that you mention it, I did have a bunch of people in here yesterday who said they were from the writers' conference. They did a lot of shopping!" Lynn grinned.

Ellie turned the earrings over in her hand. "My friend's pair is purple with pink streaks, but these shells look slightly different. They're more like pink with purple streaks."

"Yeah, they're all different. That's why they're so unique. And this is the last one, like I said, so it's a great chance to grab it before someone else does! So, honey, would you like to try them on?" Lynn produced a mirror and put it in front of Ellie.

"Actually, I don't wear dangling earrings much," said Ellie, hastily giving the earrings back.

"OK, how about a shell pendant instead? Or a bracelet? Or a ring?" said Lynn, gesturing to the other things on display beneath the glass counter. "They're all designed exclusively for the Sunset Palms Beach Resort. They're really one-of-a-kind!"

Ellie laughed. Lynn was the best saleswoman she'd ever met—the woman just didn't give up!

"No, thanks. I'll just take the bikini and the postcards today," she said firmly.

"Well, you know, we're open seven days a week," said Lynn with a bright smile. "You come back anytime now, honey!"

When she got back to the villa, Ellie sat down to write a postcard to her parents. But after she'd written: *"Dear Mum and Dad,"* she stopped. She was stumped. She didn't know what to write. After all, she could hardly tell the truth:

"I've just arrived in Florida and Aunt Olive seems to have disappeared! Oh, and by the way, she's the chief suspect in a murder investigation too."

Aside from worrying her parents sick, it might also be unnecessary because, by the time the postcard arrived in England, Aunt Olive might have turned up and the murder might be solved. But at the same time, Ellie couldn't bring herself to lie to her parents with a breezy "*Having a great time!*" fake message and pretend that everything was fine and dandy.

She sat and chewed on the end of her pencil for half an hour before she got up on an impulse and rummaged in her bag for her phone. She'd hardly used it since arriving in Florida and she was dismayed to see that it was fairly low on battery. She should have plugged it in to charge but had completely forgotten. Still, she hoped that it would be enough for a quick call. She dialed the number, then sat listening to the phone ring.

"Hello?"

"Dad!" said Ellie, breaking into a smile. Much as she found her parents frustrating at times, she realized suddenly that she missed them. It was good to hear her father's voice. "It's me—Ellie!"

"Of course, I know it's you," said her father. "Hang on while I tell your mother. She'll want to get on the extension."

A minute later, Mrs. Bishop's voice came on the line. "Ellie? Ellie, love—how are you?"

"I'm fine, Mum," said Ellie, surprised to find her voice catching slightly in her throat. Suddenly, in spite of the dazzling sunshine and beautiful beach and other wonders of Florida, she felt a pang of homesickness. She almost wanted to be back home in her parents' house, having breakfast and being lectured to and nagged at.

"So how's Florida?" asked her father. "I saw on the telly that the weather there is lovely."

"Yes, it is."

"And the resort?" asked her mother. "Is it everything you were hoping for? Beautiful beach and all?"

"Yes... yes, it's all great," mumbled Ellie.

"And how's Olive?" asked Mr. Bishop. "Is that mad sister of mine behaving herself?"

"Actually..." Ellie hesitated, then she burst out: "Dad, she's gone missing!"

"Pardon?"

Quickly, Ellie told them everything that had happened since she had arrived at Tampa Airport. They listened in silence, then at the end, her father said:

"Well, I do hope they solve the murder quickly. Nasty business, that. You're best not to get mixed up in it, Ellie."

"But Dad—"

"And as for Olive, I wouldn't worry too much about her."

"What... what do you mean?" asked Ellie, surprised. "Aren't you concerned that she's disappeared?"

"Oh, Olive is always doing things like that. Going off somewhere for days and not telling anyone. Very careless and impulsive, she is."

"Yes, remember the time she just decided to catch a flight to Alaska, David?" said Mrs. Bishop, tutting.

"Just because she got it into her head that she wanted to see the Northern Lights, ride on a dog sled, and meet a moose!"

"Yes, and she didn't see fit to tell us, even though we were planning a birthday party for her that weekend," said Mr. Bishop, sounding like he was still annoyed years later. "She just took off on the Friday night with never a word to anyone. It was only when you tried to ring her, Margaret, to ask her what flavor cake she liked that she let slip that she was on the other side of the Atlantic!" He grumbled to himself, then said to Ellie, "So don't worry, love. I'm sure your aunt is fine. She's just gone off on some madcap scheme as usual."

"But, Dad, how do you know that? What if this is different? What if this time, something bad *has* happened to her?"

"I know my sister," said Mr. Bishop. "Trust me, Ellie. She'll turn up soon, right as rain, and wonder what all the fuss was about."

Ellie hung up several minutes later, after chatting with her parents a bit longer, and sat back to stare thoughtfully into space. Maybe her parents were right. Maybe she was overreacting about Aunt Olive.

Well, I've told the police and reported her as a Missing Person, so I've done all I can for now, she thought. *So maybe I should calm down a bit now and wait and see. Give it another day or two. Maybe Dad's right and Aunt Olive will just turn up on her own.*

CHAPTER FIFTEEN

Late that evening, Ellie wandered down to the lobby bar. Although she'd had lunch hours ago and it was well past dinnertime, she wasn't really hungry. Her appetite still seemed to be messed up by jet lag. But she didn't want to sit by herself in the villa either. So she decided to grab a seat at the lobby bar and wile away a bit of time sipping a cocktail and people-watching.

When Ellie got to the bar, she found it buzzing. There was a large crowd of people, mostly women, milling around the counter, talking and laughing together. She recognized them as writers from the conference—she'd met several the night before. A few of them were discussing the talks and workshops they'd attended during the day, but most of them seemed to be gossiping about Lillian Fox's murder.

"My money is on Cheryl Jackson. I'm sure she's involved," one woman was saying.

Her friend nodded. "Yeah, she hated Lillian's guts."

"But you don't really think she could commit murder?" asked a third woman.

"I think that woman could do anything."

"Did you go to the Midwest conference back in July?" the first woman asked. "They were supposed to be on a panel together and at the last minute, the organizers changed things: they thought that having both Cheryl and Lillian would be redundant, so they decided to drop Cheryl and keep Lillian. Oh my God, you should have seen Cheryl's face that night!"

Her friend nodded again. "Oh yeah, I was there! She looked like she wanted to kill Lillian in cold blood!"

The third woman dropped her voice to a hushed tone. "What about this time? Did anyone see Cheryl leave the party on the night that Lillian was murdered?"

There were headshakes all around.

"I saw her standing by Lillian though," said the first woman. "She was listening to Lillian tell a story about how the publishers had wined and dined her at the best restaurant in town. Cheryl looked like she'd sucked on a lemon!"

They all giggled, then the first woman added: "And you know what? I just remembered that Cheryl's room is at the end of my row, right down by the beach. She could have pretended to go back to her room, then gone out through her terrace and doubled back around. All she had to do was creep around the pool—which would've been totally deserted by then—and she'd be able to get to Lillian's villa without anyone seeing her!"

Her friend squealed. "Oh my God, do you think that's what happened?"

"Well, personally, I think Lillian had it coming to her," said a new woman, joining their group.

"What do you mean?" the first three said in unison.

"Karma," said the new woman. "What goes around comes around, that's what I always say. And Lillian's treated a lot of people pretty badly. I don't just mean a few nasty words here and there—I mean some really dirty tricks."

"Ooh, I've heard those rumors too," said the first woman. "I've heard some people say Lillian Fox doesn't really write her own books, and others say that she buys reviews, and some even say she's into blackmail!"

"Blackmail?" gasped the others.

The first woman nodded. "Yeah. They said you had to be really careful what you said to Lillian 'cos she kept a record of everything. She was always hunting for stuff she could leverage later."

"Yeah, I heard that too," said the new woman. "I've always been really careful what I say around her. I know lots of people suck up to her, but I've always been a bit wary."

"Well, you know what they say about the path to success being littered with dead bodies," said the first woman with a meaningful look.

"Literally in this case!" said one of the other women.

They all laughed, then they broke off as they suddenly realized that Ellie was standing next to them, listening avidly. They turned to look coldly at her. Ellie flushed and hastily turned away. She climbed onto a stool next to the bar counter, grabbed a cocktail menu, and made a big show of reading it.

"Can I buy you a drink?"

Ellie looked up to see Blake Thornton leaning against the bar next to her. He was dressed in a white polo shirt, which showed off his deep tan, and beige chinos which accentuated the length of his legs. His sun-streaked brown hair looked damp, as if he'd recently had a shower, and he smelled faintly of a spicy male aftershave. He was easily the most gorgeous man at the bar.

Ellie realized that she was staring and dropped her gaze back down to the menu. "Oh... erm... thanks. That's really kind of you."

"So what will you have? There are specials up on the blackboard too," Blake added, nodding to a wall nearby. "And they're pretty good about getting creative here and offering something more sophisticated than the usual piña colada." He ran his eye down the list on the blackboard. "How about a vanilla chai vodka? Or a lychee martini? Or if you want something vintage, how about an Airmail? Golden rum, lime juice, honey, and Brut champagne... they even garnish it with a postage stamp, just like the old days."

"No thanks, I'd like a piña colada," said Ellie with a defiant grin. "Yes, I know it's the ultimate cheesy tourist drink and you can make fun of me all you want, but I like it and I'm not going to drink something else just to look 'cool.'"

Blake chuckled and looked at her appreciatively. "I like a lady who knows her mind and isn't afraid to be herself."

He turned away to the bartender to order the drinks. Ellie shifted uncomfortably on her stool. She hadn't thought that she would meet Blake at the bar, and now she wished that she had dressed with more care when she left the villa. She'd just thrown on a cotton blouse and a pair of cropped pants, and she hadn't even bothered to brush her hair. She leaned to one side and surreptitiously tried to catch her reflection in the glass panels on the wall behind the bar counter. *Oh my God, is that a pimple on my nose?*

"Here you go."

Ellie jerked back around and took the big frothy cocktail Blake handed to her, hoping that he hadn't seen her making faces at herself. "Uh... thanks." She looked at the glass he was holding, which held a sparkling clear liquid, together with ice and mint leaves. "What cocktail is that?"

He laughed. "It's actually a virgin mojito. I'm on call tonight so I can't drink. But this is pretty nice—very refreshing."

They sipped their drinks silently for a few moments, then Blake asked: "How's your foot?"

"Oh... it's fine. I'd actually completely forgotten about it," admitted Ellie, lifting up one foot and rotating her ankle. "The cut seems to have healed up very quickly."

"Good. And how are you enjoying Florida so far?"

"Well, other than the fact that I stumbled on a dead body on my first night in the resort and my aunt seems to have gone missing, I'm having a brilliant time," said Ellie with a wry smile.

Blake looked concerned. "Your aunt has gone missing?"

Ellie took a deep breath and told him everything that happened. It was a relief to finally have someone to confide in, to discuss all her thoughts and worries. Blake was a good listener—perhaps it was his doctor's training—and when she finally finished, Ellie felt a lot better.

"I'm not sure what to do now," said Ellie fretfully. "I've reported Aunt Olive as missing to the police, but they seem to be taking it totally the wrong way. I can't believe that they really think my aunt could be the murderer!"

"Do you think that there is a connection though? I'm not saying that your aunt killed Lillian," said Blake hastily as Ellie bristled. "I just mean, some other connection. It does seem to be a weird coincidence that the two events happened at the same time."

"Yes," said Ellie with a sigh. "Yes, I wouldn't admit it to the police, but I do think there is some kind of connection. I just don't know what! But I feel like, if I could just figure out who killed Lillian, I might be able to find out what happened to my aunt as well."

"Well, if you need any help," said Blake, "you know where my clinic is."

"Thanks, that's really nice of you," said Ellie, smiling at him.

"How long are you planning to stay in Florida?" he asked.

Ellie shrugged. "I don't know—I don't have any firm plans. My aunt had invited me to stay as long as I like. I think she was planning to spend Christmas and New Year here, and I was thinking I might do the same. But, of course, that was all before she disappeared. Now I don't know..." She sighed, then took a deep breath and sat up straighter. "Anyway, let's forget it for a while. So how about you? Are you a Florida native?"

Blake shook his head. "No, I was born up north but my family moved around a lot as I was growing up. I came to Florida to do my residency and I ended up staying here. I worked as an ER physician in a busy hospital in Miami for a couple of years, actually."

"Oh! That must have been a bit different from

being a resort doctor."

Blake burst out laughing. "'*A bit different*?' You English people and your understatements! Yeah, it was like another life." He leaned back and took a swallow of his drink. "There are only so many gunshot wounds, stabbings, and drug overdoses you can cope with before you burn out. For me, anyway. I started thinking I needed a change. Then it so happened that I met the owner of this place while he was down in Miami for a business trip. He had a heart attack and was brought into the ER, and that's how we met. We started talking and he told me about his ambitions to have a full-time resort doctor, and asked me outright if I'd be interested."

Blake shook his head and laughed. "It sure wasn't what I'd planned for myself when I studied medicine in college, but I guess life has a way of surprising you sometimes. And I *have* been surprised by how satisfying the work is. Sure, when you're pumping stomachs or stopping a major hemorrhage at a hospital, you know you're saving someone's life; but managing diabetes and child asthma symptoms out here is just as important. And there's something really nice about the slower pace and the family atmosphere of the resort. You really get to talk to people, you know, rather than see them as just organs and bodies."

"Wow," said Ellie. "I'm quite envious of you in a way. You've figured out exactly what you want in life and your career. I still haven't got a clue! It's part of the reason I came out here, you know. I wanted to get away from home and have an adventure." She laughed ruefully. "Bloody hell, I sure found it! Murder and missing persons and everything!"

"So where's home?" asked Blake. "You're British, right?"

Ellie nodded. "London. Born there and never really left. Well, other than for short trips to Europe. This is my—"

She was interrupted by the sound of loud beeping coming from Blake's pocket. He pulled his phone out and glanced at it, then gave Ellie an apologetic look. "Sorry. That's the pager app. Duty calls."

"Oh." Ellie felt a stab of disappointment. She hadn't realized how much she was enjoying his company. She held up her cocktail. "Well, thanks for the drink."

"Anytime." Blake looked down at her, his brown eyes twinkling. "I've really enjoyed our chat. I'd love to do it again sometime."

"How about tomorrow night?" Ellie surprised herself by blurting out.

Blake's smile widened. "Sure. Sounds great. Same time, same place? Or how about we get a bite to eat first? I know a place that does awesome grouper sandwiches; it's just a short walk from here. I'm not on call tomorrow night so I can leave the resort. Let's say... seven-thirty? Meet in the lobby?"

Blake left the bar a few minutes later and Ellie watched him go with mixed feelings. *What on earth were you thinking?* she berated herself. *You're only here on vacation!* Well, it was too late to pull out of the date now without seeming rude. *But one date is as far as it goes,* she told herself firmly. The last thing she needed was to get involved with someone, no matter how cute he was!

CHAPTER SIXTEEN

Ellie didn't sleep well that night. She managed to drift off around midnight but was suddenly wide awake again a couple of hours later. She rose on her elbow and glanced at the bedside clock, which read: *2:15 a.m.*

Bloody jet lag! she thought as she flopped back on her pillow and tried to get comfortable again. She tossed and turned for another hour before finally dozing off again, and then she had weird dreams. She dreamt about pirates stealing her aunt away and handsome doctors with parrots on their shoulders. When she was woken at last by a ray of sunshine stealing between the curtains, she was bleary-eyed and in a bad mood.

All she wanted to do was turn over and burrow under the blankets again, but when Ellie saw that it was nearly nine o'clock, she dragged herself out of bed and into the shower. She'd read somewhere that the best way to get over jet lag was to get into a good routine. Besides, her stomach was rumbling and she was pleased to be getting her appetite back at last, so she wanted to catch the breakfast buffet.

Ellie arrived at the *Gulf Breeze Café*—the hotel's all-day restaurant—to find it buzzing with guests. People were lining up at the buffet and eagerly helping themselves from the smorgasbord of food on offer. There were mounds of crispy bacon alongside sautéed mushrooms, roasted tomatoes, and creamy scrambled eggs, soft buttermilk pancakes with rich maple syrup, golden hash browns and fried potatoes, baskets of freshly baked bagels, muffins and pastries, flavored yogurts, fresh fruit salad, and more.

Ellie's eyes nearly popped out. She had never seen so much food in one place in her life! It all looked incredible and she was suddenly starving. She almost grabbed a plate to join the line before she remembered that she had to pick a table first. Turning, she surveyed the restaurant. There was an interior dining room, but most people were choosing to sit on the large wooden deck outside, with views straight out over the beach.

Ellie went out to join them and was just about to sit down at the nearest empty table when she heard a familiar loud squawking. She looked up to see Hemingway the scarlet macaw perched on a stand in one corner of the deck. He was surrounded by children who were laughing and pointing to him as he held nuts in one claw and cracked them with his beak.

Not everyone seemed to be so amused with the parrot though. Ellie noticed a woman sitting at a table near the stand who winced every time Hemingway squawked loudly. It was Ann, Ellie realized. Obviously, the young woman hadn't forgotten her last encounter with the macaw and she was keeping a wary eye on him as she ate.

On an impulse, Ellie walked over to Ann's table and asked brightly: "Hi! Mind if I join you?"

"Oh, sure... of course," said Ann, indicating the empty chair next to her.

Ellie sat down and, as a waiter filled her cup with hot coffee, she studied the other woman surreptitiously. Ann looked like she hadn't been sleeping well either. There were dark circles under her eyes and worry lines on her forehead. She looked like she was under some kind of strain. *Is it just the excitement of the conference,* Ellie wondered, *or is it because of a guilty conscience?* She hadn't forgotten the earring she'd found by the bamboo screen on Lillian Fox's private terrace. Had Ann dropped that? Had she been skulking around Lillian's villa that night? Ellie felt a bit guilty that she still hadn't handed the earring over to the police, but she wanted to talk to Ann first before she did something which might get the young woman in trouble. *Well, now's my chance*, thought Ellie.

"You look tired," she said to Ann, giving her a sympathetic smile. "Have you been having trouble sleeping? I've really been struggling because of the jet lag, but I don't suppose you would have that problem? Have you come from very far?"

"Not as far as England! I live in Pennsylvania," said Ann.

"Oh, then is it the murder?" Ellie said chattily. "I've found it a bit disturbing too! It's just so surreal to think that someone was murdered, right here, right under our noses, isn't it? I mean, that's the kind of thing you expect to see on TV and in movies!"

"Yeah, I suppose so," said Ann.

"The police must have had loads of questions for you, huh? I mean, they asked *me* loads of questions, and I didn't even really know Lillian. I'll bet you could tell them a lot more about her."

Ann shifted nervously in her seat. "What d'you mean?"

"Oh, you know, because you're a writer and you knew Lillian and spent time with her at conferences and stuff."

"I never hung out with Lillian," said Ann quickly. "I barely knew her."

"But I thought, since you pointed her out to me that night... and I heard that she used to mentor new authors, didn't she? So I thought she might have helped you."

Ann flushed. "No, she never helped me."

"That's weird," said Ellie, pretending to look puzzled. "Because I heard someone say they saw you going to Lillian's villa on the night of the murder and I thought you must have been going there to ask her advice about something."

Ann went pale. "Wh-who said that?"

"Oh, just one of the resort staff I was talking to yesterday," said Ellie airily. "He was passing by the pool that night and he saw you heading to Lillian's villa. It was just a short while before her body was found, actually..."

"It wasn't... I mean, I didn't..." Ann stammered. "Yes... erm... now that you mention it, I did go to see Lillian that night. I wanted to ask her about a book idea I had. But she didn't answer the door."

"Did you hear anyone inside?"

Ann shook her head. "No, although I might have missed something. There was a TV on in the villa next door. It was really loud and sort of drowned everything else out."

That would have been me, thought Ellie guiltily as she recalled turning up the volume on the sitcom she had been watching.

"Anyway, I tried knocking a few more times but when I didn't get any response, I went back to my own room," said Ann.

"And you only went up to Lillian's door at the front of the villa? You didn't go around to her terrace at the back?"

"No, of course not. Why would I do that?"

Ellie shrugged. "I don't know... Maybe you thought you could peek in her windows or something."

"I wouldn't do that!" cried Ann indignantly. "Why would you think that I'd gone around the back?"

"Because I found your earrings on Lillian's terrace," said Ellie. "Or at least, one of your earrings. The one that Hemingway didn't yank out of your ear earlier that evening."

Ann threw an involuntary glance at the parrot and her hands went unconsciously to her earlobes. This morning, she was wearing another set of dangling earrings shaped like two strawberries.

"No, you must be mistaken," she said. "It can't have been my earring. I never went around the back to Lillian's terrace."

"I know what I picked up and it definitely looked like your earring," insisted Ellie.

"Well, it couldn't have been mine. Maybe... maybe it belonged to someone else," said Ann.

"Someone with the same earring?" said Ellie skeptically.

"Yes, why not? I bought those shell earrings from the gift shop. Anyone else could have bought a pair too." She looked at Ellie. "You still don't believe me, do you? I can show you the other one if you want."

"The other one?"

"Yeah, the other earring. The one that Hemingway didn't grab. That's the one that you think I dropped, right? I've got it back in my room. If you want to come with me after breakfast, I can show you—"

"Uh... no, no, that's not necessary," said Ellie, feeling embarrassed now. "Sorry, Ann, I didn't mean to accuse you. I'm sure you can't have murdered Lillian! It's just that... well, it was a weird coincidence finding that earring and remembering that you had the same one."

"Someone else must have bought the same earrings from the gift shop," repeated Ann.

"Yes, you're right," Ellie agreed. "I wish I knew who!"

"Have you told the police about the earring?" asked Ann.

"No, not yet, but I'm going to. I probably should have given it to them already, but I wanted to speak to you first."

"Oh. Thanks, that was really nice of you." Ann gave her a grateful smile. Then she indicated the buffet. "You have to try some of their bacon. It's absolutely delicious!"

"I can't wait," said Ellie, eying the things on the other girl's plate with relish. She stood up from the table. "A full American breakfast—here I come!"

CHAPTER SEVENTEEN

After breakfast, Ellie was so stuffed that she could barely walk. Ann invited her to join her at a talk entitled "Writing Strong Female Characters" but Ellie thought she'd simply fall asleep if she sat down in a darkened conference room! So she waved goodbye to her new friend and went off by herself.

She decided to wander around and explore the grounds. This way, at least, she would work off a bit of her breakfast. The Sunset Palms Beach Resort was much larger than she'd realized, with extensive gardens and leisure facilities, plus an area of sand dunes and natural vegetation along the shoreline adjoining the beach. At any other time, Ellie would have enjoyed roaming the landscaped gardens, filled with lush greenery and native birds, or making use of the tennis courts, mini-golf course, watersports rentals, or the dozen other activities on offer—or even just flopping into one of the conveniently placed hammocks and enjoying the view of the beach and the sparkling blue water beyond.

But with everything that was going on, Ellie just couldn't think about enjoying herself. She sighed and wandered half-heartedly down a path leading to the beach. If only Aunt Olive were here, how things would be different! Her aunt loved to sightsee and explore, and was always fun and spontaneous. She would probably have been dragging Ellie to every local attraction or chartering a private boat to go out on the water.

Wait a minute... Ellie stopped suddenly. Thinking of private boat charters made her remember what Nancy had told her yesterday. She had wanted to ask Nancy more about the tour operator who had been recommended to Aunt Olive, but Mr. Anderson, the hotel manager, had interrupted them and things had gotten sidetracked.

Ellie spun around and began marching back toward the main resort building. When she got to the lobby, she went up to the reception. A different girl was there today. Ellie asked her about the resort chauffeur, hoping that Nancy wasn't out on a job.

"Nancy? Hmm, let me see..." The girl tapped on her keyboard and checked her computer screen. "She's got an airport job booked for this afternoon, but she should still be here at the resort." She glanced up and looked around the lobby. "Nancy often hangs out around the lobby. If she's not here, then she's probably in her office."

"Where's that?" Ellie asked.

"It's the Resort Travel & Transport Hut," said the girl. "It's actually near the pool deck, just a bit beyond the Tiki Bar. There's a small hut there with a thatched roof. There's a sign on the outside."

"Thanks," said Ellie.

When she got to the pool deck, she was surprised to see that it wasn't as busy today, then she remembered that it wasn't the weekend anymore. Many of the families with children must have gone home and the writers were probably at their talks and workshops, so the whole outdoor area around the pool was relatively quiet.

Ellie walked around the large, kidney-shaped pool, past the Tiki Bar, and found a small, thatched-roof hut tucked under some leaning palm trees. There was a large sign with the words "Resort Travel & Transport" hanging in one of the windows and when she pushed the door open, she found herself inside a very modern-looking interior. There was a little waiting area with seats and large racks of brochures advertising local attractions, and then a door leading to an inner office. The door was slightly ajar and when Ellie knocked, she heard Nancy's voice say: "Come in!"

She stepped in to find Nancy seated behind a large desk, sorting through some files. The chauffeur looked up and her face broke into a smile as she saw

Ellie.

"Well, hello! Nice to see you, Ellie. Are you looking to book a ride?"

"No, actually, I was hoping you could help me with some information," said Ellie, dropping into the chair facing Nancy's desk. "You know, yesterday when you said Aunt Olive was asking you about fast boats— you said you'd recommended someone to her. Can you give me his name, please? I thought I'd try to call him and see if my aunt *has* contacted him. Maybe he'll know more about any plans she might have had or be able to give me a lead..."

"Oh sure. His name's Earl—Earl Stone." She opened a drawer behind the desk and took out a thick file, which she opened and began flipping through. "In fact, I'll give you our whole list of local tour operators. This is what I gave your aunt, so you've got all the names and contact details, in case she went with someone else. They've all got private boats that can be chartered, and some of them run small group outings, day trips, that kind of thing, down to Fort Myers or Sarasota, or all the way down to Key West..." She stopped at a page and turned the file around 180 degrees so that Ellie could read the list. "You can copy down their numbers if you want. But you're right, a good place to start would be with Earl. He's this one here."

As Ellie was copying the numbers, Nancy snapped her fingers and said, "You know what? I just remembered—Earl had a bunch of leaflets printed and he gave me some the last time I saw him. Hang on a minute, I'll see if I've still got them…"

She went out to the waiting area, where she rummaged through the racks of brochures. "Ah! Here it is!" she said at last. She came back in and handed Ellie a long, rectangular leaflet.

Ellie looked down at the picture on the leaflet, which showed a rugged-looking man in his sixties, with long gray hair and a clipped beard. He was wearing a white T-shirt and faded jeans, rolled up to the knees, and he was squinting as he looked out to sea. He was standing on the deck of a powerful-looking motor yacht, and in one hand he was holding an enormous fish caught on a hook.

Nancy looked down at the leaflet as well and said: "You could do worse than hire Earl for a day trip yourself! He knows the whole coast like the back of his hand, and he used to live down in the Keys for several years. He's always full of stories."

"I'll call him as soon as I get back to my room," Ellie said.

"Don't worry if you have trouble getting through to him," said Nancy. "Earl is a law unto himself and he can be really difficult to get hold of sometimes. He often doesn't answer his phone, especially when he's out in the boat, and he can head out to sea for days. He's nothing like the other tour operators—you'd think he would have trouble with an attitude like that, but he's still really popular. Can you believe it?"

Ellie glanced down at the photo again. "Well, he

looks like such a character, people probably find him fascinating," she said with a laugh.

Nancy nodded. "Yup, that's it. It's not just about making money for him. A lot of the time, these tourist outfits are all about the numbers, you know? Just trying to pack in as many as possible—but Earl's different. Anyway, if you can't get hold of him on the phone, you might want to try and catch him in person."

"How do I do that? Do you know where I can find him?" Ellie asked.

"Now that's a question! He sleeps on his boat, and like I said, he does things by his own schedule so he never really has a set routine. If he feels like taking off for a few days, he'll do that and nobody can get hold of him." Nancy shook her head with a mixture of admiration and exasperation. "But if he's not out on the water, then you might find him at the Sunset Palms Marina. That's on the Intracoastal, across from the beach."

"Is that near the resort?" asked Ellie. "What's the Intracoastal?"

"You know we're on a barrier island, right?" Nancy said, seeing Ellie's confused look. "There's a strip of long, narrow islands that hug the coast of the Pinellas County peninsula. You've got Honeymoon Island and Clearwater Beach farther north and then, after us, it goes all the way down to Long Key and Mullet Key in the south. The water between the islands and the main peninsula is called the

Intracoastal Waterway. It's joined to the Gulf by inlets between the islands."

"Oh... I didn't realize. I thought the resort was on the mainland."

"Yeah, the geography is a little unique here."

"So that's why we seemed to drive over so many bridges on the day I arrived!" said Ellie, remembering.

"Yup, we had to cross Tampa Bay to get onto the main peninsula, and then cross the Intracoastal again to get onto the barrier islands." Nancy gestured out the window. "The beach here is on the side of the island facing the Gulf, and on the other side, which faces the Intracoastal, there's the Sunset Palms Marina. It's not as big as the one up at Clearwater. That's a real treat to visit, especially Pier 60. But our marina is pretty cool too. Earl has his boat moored there when he's on shore."

"Can I walk there?"

"You could, although it's a pretty long way on foot—the boulevard is very wide and then you've got to walk across the island to the marina. You might get hot and tired. I'd be happy to take you, honey. It's only a short drive."

"Thanks. I'll try giving Earl a ring first and see if I can get hold of him that way," said Ellie. She stood up with a sigh. "I really hope he'll be able to tell me something about my aunt."

Nancy gave her a sympathetic look. "You making any progress?" she asked.

Ellie shook her head. "No, nothing. It's so frustrating and worrying!"

"I'm sure your aunt's fine," said Nancy in a consoling voice. "She'll probably turn up when you least expect it." She paused, then added: "You really don't think your aunt had anything to do with the murder?"

CHAPTER EIGHTEEN

Ellie stiffened. But Nancy seemed genuinely curious—she wasn't some journalist trying to get a sensationalist story. So Ellie relaxed again and said: "I'm positive my aunt had nothing to do with the murder."

"Well, who do you think committed the murder then? One of the other guests?"

"Maybe. Or it could be one of the resort staff."

"Really?" said Nancy, looking startled. "Who?"

Ellie hesitated. She hadn't even thought through her own theory properly yet and she wasn't sure she should have been discussing it with anyone. On the other hand, Nancy was easy to talk to and it was a nice to have a friendly ear.

"Well, there's a guy who works at the Tiki Bar. He seems to be very friendly with the ladies and I heard a rumor that Lillian was sleeping with him."

"Ah, I think you mean Paolo, our resident Casanova," said Nancy, smirking.

"But I don't think it's him, actually," said Ellie. "Although it could be his girlfriend."

"His girlfriend?"

"She's one of the maids," Ellie explained. "She cleans Lillian's villa—and my aunt's too. That's how I met her."

"But why do you think she could be involved?"

"I... erm... overheard her and Paolo talking," said Ellie, not really wanting to admit that she had been sneaking up on people and eavesdropping on their conversation. "Maria sounded really jealous of Lillian, and she wasn't in her room on the night of the murder. Paolo said he went to look for her but she wasn't there. She told him she went for a walk because she couldn't sleep but I think that sounds very suspicious."

"Wow," said Nancy. "So you think it's one of them?"

Ellie shrugged. "I don't know. It could also be a guest. For example, one of the writers from the conference. There's a woman called Cheryl Jackson who was really jealous of Lillian. In fact, listening to the gossip, it sounds like she hated Lillian's guts. She's furious because Lillian stole her crown in the romance writing community and also got a book deal with her publishers." Ellie frowned. "The thing is, I don't think the earring belongs to her."

"What earring?"

"I found an earring on Lillian's terrace on the night that she was killed. I thought it belonged to one of the other writers—this girl called Ann. I got talking to her at the welcome party in *Hammerheads Bar and Grill* on the night of the murder. She was wearing a pair of earrings exactly like the one I found," said Ellie. "Hemingway grabbed one and flew off with it, but she still had the other one, and I thought that was what I found on Lillian's terrace."

"You *thought*?" Nancy frowned. "You mean you don't think so anymore?"

"Well... I asked Ann about the earring this morning and she said that she was never on Lillian's terrace. She says that she went to ask Lillian some advice about writing but Lillian never answered her door, so Ann gave up and left. She swears that she didn't go around to the back of the villa and onto the terrace—"

"But couldn't she be lying? Why else would you have found her earring there?"

"Well, Ann said it wasn't hers. She said it belonged to someone else—which could be true, I suppose. I mean, the earrings *are* from the gift shop, and Lynn the shopkeeper told me that they were really popular, so I suppose anyone in the resort could have bought a pair. Plus, Ann said she still had her other one; she offered to show it to me. So if she's still got it, the one I picked up can't be hers."

"Hmm..." Nancy looked thoughtful. "So you're not

gonna tell the police about it?"

Ellie fidgeted with her hands. "I don't know... I like Ann. She seems like such a sweet girl, really shy and insecure. I don't want to make trouble for her. Besides, I couldn't think of any reason why she would want to kill Lillian Fox. I mean, if it had been Cheryl Jackson, that would have made perfect sense. But Ann? She knew Lillian but she wasn't really in the same circle. She just sort of worshipped Lilian from afar. So I can't understand why she would want to kill her! You'd think she would want to keep Lillian alive, because she might be able to get advice and mentoring from her..."

Ellie took a deep breath, then sighed and said, "Still, I suppose it's evidence in a murder investigation and I should really hand it in. Let the police deal with it. They can question Ann again or try to find out who really owns the earring—"

"Maybe you shouldn't rush to do anything," said Nancy. "I mean, if you're wrong about Ann, she could end up in a lot of trouble for nothing. And if it leaked out to the media, it could end up being really unpleasant for her. Even if she's innocent... you know, mud sticks and all that. If she's just a new author, starting out, that could really wreck her chances of getting published."

"Yes, you're right. That's why I've been dragging my heels," said Ellie. "I don't want to get an innocent person in trouble and I certainly don't want Ann to have to deal with press attention." She shuddered as she remembered her encounter with Ted Baxter of the *Tampa Daily News*. "Poor thing, it would be horrible for her. And Ann was so kind and friendly to me that first night, when I was all alone and didn't know anyone. It feels really wrong, almost like I'm betraying her, if I go and snitch on her to the police."

"Maybe you should sleep on it," Nancy suggested. "My grandma always used to say: 'Things always look clearer in the morning.' You've waited this long to tell the police. Another day won't make a difference."

"That's a good idea," said Ellie, smiling gratefully at the older woman. "Thanks, Nancy! I feel much better having talked to you." She held up the leaflet. "Can I take this?"

"Oh sure. I have several copies. Good luck getting hold of Earl, and remember, if you need someone to drive you to the marina, just give me a holler."

CHAPTER NINETEEN

Ellie left the Resort Travel & Transport Hut and walked across the pool deck. The lounges chairs and cabanas were filled with people this morning, stretched out sunbathing, dozing, reading books, or scrolling on their phones and iPads. The sun was beating down strongly but there was a lovely breeze coming off the sea, and the cabanas looked very inviting with their plump cushions and wide circular mattresses.

Maybe I'll go and change into my new bikini and come out here to the pool, thought Ellie. *But first, I must try to get hold of Earl and ask if Aunt Olive contacted him.* She had meant to buy a local SIM card for her cell phone but hadn't gotten around to it yet; so it was still better for her to use the landline in her villa for a local number, rather than calling from her phone, which was roaming on a U.K. network.

Ellie tried Earl's number as soon as she got back to the villa but the ringing went unanswered until it jumped to voicemail. She decided to change and then try again. She stripped off and wriggled into her new bikini, then stood in front of the mirror admiring it. She was delighted that it looked as good as it had in the shop. She pulled an oversized T-shirt on top, thinking to herself that the next time she stopped by the gift shop, she would pick up a sarong. Then she grabbed her sunglasses and floppy hat, some toiletries, and a few other necessities, and stuffed everything into the beach tote that Aunt Olive had left for her.

Pausing by the phone in the living room, Ellie tried Earl Stone's number again, but once more the phone rang unanswered. *Well, Nancy did warn me*, she thought. Deciding to try later when she returned from the pool, Ellie grabbed her beach tote and headed out. As she was locking her front door, however, she noticed that the door of the villa next door was slightly ajar. She frowned. Was someone in Lillian's villa? But it was still supposed to be off-limits. The yellow crime-scene tape was still stretched across the doorway. Perhaps the police had come back to check something?

Curious, Ellie went over and pushed the door open even more, straining her ears to listen for voices. But she couldn't hear anything except a strange fumbling, rustling sound. *What is that?* She hesitated, then ducked under the crime-scene tape and stepped into the villa. Quietly, she tiptoed down the hallway and into the main living area. It was empty. But there were sounds coming from one of the bedrooms.

Ellie tiptoed past the kitchenette and couches, which were a mirror image of the ones in her aunt's villa, and paused in the corridor which led to the two bedrooms. She heard an exclamation of frustration and then a voice cursing softly. It seemed to be coming from the en suite bathroom in the master bedroom. When Ellie tiptoed through the bedroom and peered in the bathroom, she found a woman hunched over the vanity, rummaging through Lillian's make-up bags and toiletries.

It was Cheryl Jackson!

"What are you doing?" Ellie asked.

Cheryl gasped and whirled around. Hastily, she dropped the make-up bag she had been holding and backed away from the vanity.

"I... erm... I was just..." she stammered. Then she cleared her throat and said, "I... I was looking for my... erm... lipstick."

Ellie raised her eyebrows. "*Your* lipstick? In Lillian Fox's cosmetic bag?"

Cheryl flushed. "I thought Lillian might have taken it by mistake. We... we went to the restroom at the same time during one of the workshops and we were touching up our make-up in front of the mirror next to each other. So... erm... this morning, when I couldn't find my lipstick, I thought Lillian might have picked up my lipstick by mistake and put it in her make-up bag. So I came over to check."

Hah! A likely story, thought Ellie. It was so obvious that Cheryl had been snooping in Lillian's room. In fact, she had looked like she was desperately looking for something. The question was, what was it?

"Well, it looks like the lipstick's not here," said Cheryl brightly, edging out of the bathroom. "I guess I must have left it somewhere else. I've got to run now—I'm chairing a panel this afternoon and I have to prepare my notes!"

Without waiting for a reply, she hurried from the room, and Ellie heard the front door slam. She turned to look at the vanity, frowning. What had Cheryl really been looking for? She walked back out into Lillian's bedroom and looked around. There were clothes pulled out of drawers and things tipped out of the suitcases. She didn't know if this was the result of the police search and sweep by the forensic team, or if it was Cheryl's handiwork.

Ellie let herself out of Lillian's villa and made her way to the pool. It was nearly midday now and the area around the deck was mobbed by people trying to escape the heat with cooling dips in the aquamarine water. The cabana that she had been eying up earlier was taken and there were no others available, so Ellie had to make do with a lounge chair. But it was very comfortable too and she stretched out luxuriously, enjoying the feel of the hot sun on her bare skin.

Soon she began to feel drowsy and, before she knew it, Ellie had drifted off to sleep. She was startled awake by the sound of a shriek and sat up quickly on the lounge, looking wildly around. Then she realized that it was just a child screaming in play; she could see a family in the pool, splashing each other.

Relaxing back on the lounge, Ellie glanced at her watch and was surprised to see that she had dozed off for a couple of hours. She was glad that she'd remembered to apply sunscreen—even so, her skin looked quite pink and her arms had already started to freckle. Ellie yawned and stretched. She'd thought that she was over the jet lag, but it seemed that she was still more tired than she realized. She had missed lunch and realized suddenly how hungry and thirsty she was. Getting up, Ellie strolled over to the Tiki Bar, where Paolo was in his usual position, mixing cocktails.

"Hi," she said, smiling at him.

"Hel-lo," he said, flashing his brilliant smile at her. "What can I get you, ma'am?"

"Can you do a frozen daiquiri?"

"Sure can! Which flavor would you like? There's strawberry, lime, apricot, peach, blueberry, and mango-and-mint."

"Wow," said Ellie. "I always thought daiquiris were just strawberry! The mango-and-mint sounds great—I'll try that."

"Coming right up!"

Ellie watched him expertly begin to shake her cocktail and they chatted lightly about Florida, the beach, the summer weather, and other innocuous topics. She had to admit that Paolo could be really charming when he made the effort and it was obvious that he was very popular with the ladies. Several women stopped by the Tiki Bar to flirt with him. Paolo teased and bantered with them all, and Ellie could see that he was good at making every woman feel special.

When he handed her the finished drink, he reached into his shirt pocket and produced a tiny cocktail umbrella which he placed on the frozen daiquiri with a flourish. Seeing the miniature umbrella made Ellie remember the one she had seen in Lillian's hand on the night of the murder.

"Do you get those on drinks if you order them from the lobby bar? Or any of the other restaurants?"

Paolo grinned and took another paper umbrella out of his shirt pocket, opening it and twirling it to show her the design. "Nope. These are made exclusively for the Tiki Bar, see?"

Ellie saw that the words "Tiki Bar" were printed on the pink canopy of the tiny umbrella. "What about Room Service? Can you get these umbrellas if you order a cocktail to be sent to your room?"

"No, you need to come here, to the Tiki Bar," said Paolo, smirking. "Our cocktails are special and I hand out the umbrellas myself from my special stash." He tapped his shirt pocket, which was bulging with more unused paper umbrellas.

"You know, the woman who was murdered—she was clutching one of these when her body was pulled out of the pool," said Ellie.

Paolo's smile faded and his eyes turned wary. "Yeah, so?"

"Oh, I just wondered where she got it from," said Ellie innocently. "I mean, if you're saying that these umbrellas only come from your bar... then that means that she must have got it from you?"

"So what if she did? That doesn't mean that I gave it to her that night," said Paolo aggressively. "She could have saved an umbrella from a drink she had earlier in the day." He gestured at the other lounge chairs around the pool, pointing at several empty cocktail glasses, each sporting a paper umbrella. "Look around! See, there are umbrellas in practically every drink. And even if you didn't order a cocktail yourself, you could have nabbed one from an empty drink left by another guest."

He had a point, Ellie admitted. Just because Lillian had been holding a cocktail umbrella when she died didn't necessarily point the finger at him. But... it was still suspicious.

"You sound very defensive," she said to Paolo.

"I don't know what you're talking about," he snapped. His friendly, flirtatious manner had completely disappeared. "You think I had something to do with the murder? Oh, I get it. I'm a Latino guy so I have to be a criminal, right?"

"That's... that's not what I mean," said Ellie, taken aback.

Paolo started busily wiping the bar counter, even though there were no spills visible. "Did you want anything else, ma'am?" he asked in a tight voice.

"Oh yes, I'd like to order some food, please," said Ellie, grabbing the bar menu and scanning it quickly.

She ordered some shoe-string fries, then with a final troubled look at Paolo, she returned to her lounge chair to wait for her food.

CHAPTER TWENTY

As she leaned back on the lounge chair and sipped her cocktail, Ellie mulled over Paolo's behavior. He certainly acted like a man who was scared. But did that mean he'd killed Lillian Fox? After all, even if he'd simply visited Lillian on the night of her murder, he might have still been nervous about that information getting out. He had probably been the last person to see the dead woman. It would instantly make him a strong suspect.

The French fries arrived—hot, salty, and crispy—and Ellie munched them with pleasure. Her thoughts left Paolo and returned to Cheryl Jackson, who was a much more likely suspect in her mind. What had the romance writer been searching for in Lillian's room? She wasn't some random thief—Ellie had noted that Lillian's purse had been lying on the bed, with the wallet inside plainly visible. And some of the dead woman's jewelry had been carelessly thrown in an ashtray on the bedside table. No, Cheryl wasn't just a common thief, after money or valuables. She had been searching for something specific.

Maybe something that might incriminate her in the murder? thought Ellie suddenly, sitting upright.

It had to be something important for her to sneak in like that and risk getting caught. Cheryl Jackson was proud and she had a professional reputation to uphold. Ellie thought back to the writers' welcome party she'd attended. Malicious talk about Cheryl was already rampant—if anyone found out that she had broken into Lillian's room and was snooping around in there, the gossip would be really devastating.

And judging from the sounds of frustration Ellie had overheard and the way Cheryl had been cursing, it seemed that she hadn't found what she had been looking for. Ellie wished that she could discover what it was—it might've been the key to solving the whole mystery. But even if she was willing to sneak into Lillian's room again, she didn't know if she'd have any more luck than Cheryl had. The other woman seemed to have done a pretty thorough search, so whatever it was couldn't be in an easy hiding place.

At last, feeling like she was going around in circles, Ellie pushed thoughts of the murder case out of her mind. She picked up the book she had brought outside with her. It was a novel she had seen lying in one of her aunt's suitcases and now that she looked at it more closely, she saw that it was actually one of Aunt Olive's own books. It was a murder mystery set in a holiday resort in the Caribbean. Intrigued, Ellie flipped to the first page and began reading.

Aunt Olive was a good writer, and within a few moments, Ellie was engrossed in the story. She read steadily all afternoon, stopping only to order two more long, cool drinks and once to use the restroom. The sun was beginning to slide down the horizon when she finished the last chapter.

That was so clever how the detective worked things out! she thought as she closed the book and put it down. *Most people would never have thought of looking in those hiding places for the secret note—*

Ellie paused. *Wait a minute...* She grabbed the book and opened it again, flipping back until she found the right chapter. Slowly, she read, then re-read the paragraph. The detective in the story was just explaining how he had found the vital clue:

"People always use similar hiding places when they're staying in a hotel room. Everyone thinks that they're really clever, but most thieves know exactly where people hide things. There's a clichéd list of places: under the mattress, behind the TV, inside the tissue box, taped under drawers, or put in plastic bags and placed in the toilet tank. Some people are even pretty ingenious and hide things in the hem of the room curtains. But really, all these places are well-known and easily discovered. Anybody who is savvy

and really trying to hide something would never put it in any of these places. Nevertheless, when I'm searching, I always look in the places on that list first as most people are creatures of habit and tediously predictable."

Ellie dropped the book in her lap and sat up straight. Her gaze wandered across the pool to the opposite side of the deck, where the villas with private terraces were arranged in a row facing the pool. She could just see her aunt's villa, the first in the row, and Lillian's villa next to it, through the hanging fronds of a palm tree clump, which was planted next to the pool and partially blocked her view.

Ellie felt a flicker of excitement as she wondered suddenly if she should go back into Lillian's villa and try her own luck at searching. Armed with the knowledge from her aunt's novel, she might succeed where Cheryl Jackson had failed! Eagerly, she got up and began collecting her things. She glanced around: it was late in the afternoon now, and many of the families were packing up and heading back to their rooms to clean up and to get ready for dinner, so the pool area was quiet. That was good. With fewer people around, hopefully nobody would look over at Lillian's villa and notice unusual activity. The glass sliding doors which led onto the terrace were tinted for privacy anyway, so Ellie hoped that even if someone was looking in that direction, they wouldn't necessarily see someone moving around inside.

She made her way back to her own villa and pretended to take her time opening the front door. Tossing her beach bag into the hallway, Ellie leaned back out and looked up and down the corridor. There was nobody around. She shut her own door, darted across to Lillian's door, and tried the handle. As she had suspected, the latch was faulty and the lock hadn't quite engaged. That was how Cheryl Jackson had gotten into the villa earlier. Ellie checked again that the coast was clear, then opened the door and slipped inside.

She shut the door carefully behind her and stood for a moment, looking around the room, her pulse fast and excited. There were no lights on—good—but she would still take care to keep away from the sliding doors which led out onto the terrace. Even with the tinted glass, someone near the pool might see her if she went too close.

Slowly, Ellie prowled around the room, beginning a systematic search. She tried to remember what the detective in her aunt's novel had said. First, she went into Lillian's bedroom, pulled out all the drawers, and groped under them, feeling for anything taped underneath. Then she checked under the mattress and behind the headboard. Nothing. She didn't bother searching Lillian's luggage as she was sure both Cheryl and the police would have gone through that thoroughly. She did, however, check inside every pair of shoes. Next, she went into the en suite bathroom, where she looked in the toilet tank, behind the shower curtains, and even rummaged through the toiletries, opening each bottle and looking inside to make sure nothing was hidden in them. Again, nothing.

Back in the main living room, Ellie searched under the sofa and unzipped all the covers of the seat cushions, sliding her hand in to feel inside. She looked behind the TV console and the TV monitor itself, as well as the desk alongside the wall. She flipped the phone upside down and checked to see if there were any loose panels, and looked under the shade of the desk lamp. She felt the hems of the hanging curtains, checking that nothing had been slipped inside the fold of fabric at the bottom.

Starting to feel frustrated, Ellie moved on to the kitchenette, where she checked behind the fridge, peeked behind the microwave, and had a good rummage in all the cupboards. She even lifted the bag out of the garbage can under the sink and peered at the bottom of the plastic container but there was nothing there. Undaunted, Ellie turned to the entrance hallway and looked in the closet. *The ironing board!* she thought. She pulled the long, flat board out and released the clasp to unfold it. Then she slid her hand beneath the padded cover, feeling left and right. But there was nothing tucked between the board and the cover.

Disappointed, Ellie replaced the ironing board and turned back to survey the living room again. She blew out a breath of frustration. She had been so sure that she'd be able to find something! Maybe she was totally on the wrong track; maybe there was nothing to find... No, there had to be something. Otherwise, why would Cheryl Jackson have taken the risk of breaking in to search like that?

Ellie looked up and her face brightened as her eyes went up to the ceiling. There was a large light fixture in the middle of the living room, with three lamps joined together and hanging from a central cord. Each lampshade was in the shape of a conch seashell. It was obviously a theme carried on from the interior design theme of the resort lobby—Ellie remembered admiring the light fittings there, which had been chandeliers made of seashells. These were like a smaller, more practical version.

Ellie stared at the light fixture, her thoughts racing. Those conch lampshades would make a brilliant hiding place. They were high up, out of the way, so as not to catch people's attention. Housekeeping was unlikely to disturb anything by cleaning or dusting. And they were pretty inaccessible: unless you climbed up on a chair or ladder, you wouldn't be able to check the shells easily, and the hassle and effort would probably put a lot of people off...

Well, it's not going to put me *off*, thought Ellie. She looked around and grabbed one of the tall-backed dining chairs next to the small table by the kitchenette. She dragged this across the room and positioned it under the light, then climbed up to check inside each shell-shaped lampshade. Ellie wasn't particularly tall and, for a minute, she was afraid that she wouldn't be able to reach. She had to stand on tiptoe and really stretch to slide her fingers inside each conch and feel around. The first two held nothing except dust, but as she slid her finger inside the lip of the last one, she felt something small, hard, and rectangular. *Bingo!*

Ellie pulled it out and looked at it. It was a USB stick. She was just turning it over when she heard the sound of footsteps in the corridor outside the villa.

Yikes! Was someone coming in?

CHAPTER TWENTY-ONE

In a panic, Ellie jumped down from the chair and dragged it back across the room, shoving it into position next to the table. Then she looked around frantically for somewhere to hide. She heard the rumble of men's voices outside the door. One of them sounded familiar. Was it Detective Carson? *Oh my God, if the police find me in here, I'll be in serious trouble!* thought Ellie. She'd never be able to explain what she was doing in Lillian Fox's room, especially as it was still taped off as a crime scene.

Ellie started toward the bedrooms to look for somewhere to hide, but it was too late. Someone was already fumbling with the front door handle. She could hear an exclamation of surprise and dismay as the police discovered that the latch was broken. She turned and looked wildly around the living room, then dived behind the long curtains hanging on either side of the sliding glass doors which looked out onto the terrace. It was a pathetic hiding place but she had no other choice. There was nowhere else that provided any kind of cover in the living room.

Ellie shrank back against the wall, hoping that the thick folds of the curtains would be enough to hide the bulge of her body. Thankfully, they were hung a bit far out from the wall, so there was a good-spaced gap between the fabric and the wall. They were also long, with the hems skimming the floor. If she stood on tiptoe, only the tips of her toes would be showing. She was barefoot and Ellie was thankful that she hadn't had time to get a pedicure before leaving London. The carpet was a muddy beige, which blended nicely with the flesh tone of her bare toes. As long as nobody came up too close to the curtains, they wouldn't be likely to notice anything.

She pressed herself against the wall and sucked her stomach in, just as she heard the front door swing open and voices talking as people entered the villa. Through a gap in the folds, she saw two men: Detective Carson and one of his officers. They seemed to be deep in discussion about the case and barely glanced in her direction. But just when Ellie thought she could relax, Carson spoke.

"Bit stuffy in here, isn't it? Go and open the windows," he said, indicating the glass sliding doors.

Ellie froze and held her breath as the officer came over and fumbled with the catch on the doors. But to her relief, he didn't look her way. As soon as he'd slid the doors open, leaving the screen door in place, he returned to Detective Carson on the other side of the room.

Ellie let her breath out and relaxed slightly. *Whew!* It looked like she was pretty safe in this hiding place for the time being. In fact, the officer coming so close and not noticing her meant that she was very well-concealed, even at close range. As long as the detectives didn't actually pull the curtains aside, they shouldn't have any idea that she was here...

"*MIAOW!*"

Ellie jerked her head around and she saw with dismay that Mojito the resort cat was standing on the terrace, just on the other side of the screen door. From where she was standing, Mojito could see the gap between the curtains and the wall, and she had obviously noticed Ellie hiding there. The cat was twitching her tail, staring at Ellie in fascination.

"*MIAOW!*" she said again.

Ellie made a tiny shooing motion with her hand, hoping the cat might get the hint and go away, but to her horror, Mojito came closer instead, pressing her nose against the mesh and sniffing curiously. Ellie glanced back through the gap in the curtains, terrified that the detectives would notice the cat's interest and come over to investigate. They had stopped talking and were looking curiously in this direction.

"It's that damn cat," said Carson, glowering. "It was in here the other day, getting under my feet."

Mojito reached up and began clawing the mesh on the screen door.

"Hey!" cried the officer, hurrying over. "Don't do that! You'll rip it!"

He grabbed the handle to jiggle the screen door, but instead it unlatched and slid open. Instantly, Mojito slipped through the gap, darted between his legs, and trotted into the room.

"HEY!" cried the officer, lunging and trying to grab the cat.

But Mojito was too quick for him. She darted around him and jumped onto the sofa, where she settled against a cushion and began washing a paw.

"Ahh... leave it," growled Carson. "It's not getting in anyone's way on the couch." He gestured to a pile of things that he'd brought out of the bedroom and dumped on the dining table. "Come and help me look through this stuff. I've been hearing on the hotel grapevine that one of the resort staff—that good-looking Latino guy at the Tiki Bar—has got a way with the ladies. Seems like he and Lillian Fox might have had a thing going. I questioned him this morning and he acted really nervous. He says he never saw Fox that night, but I think he's lying."

"Forensics?" asked the officer.

Carson nodded. "We got samples. Forensics will be going over the evidence again to see if they can find a match. But in the meantime, let's do things the old-fashioned way: look through the woman's things. Maybe there'll be something here, like a picture of them together or something..."

The officer went over obediently and the two men huddled over the table, sifting through Lillian's personal effects. Ellie slowly released her breath again, then glanced at the screen door. The officer had left it slightly open. The gap was. just wide enough for her to squeeze through and it was only a few feet from her. It could be her escape route. But to take it, she would have to leave the cover of the curtains and her movement might attract the detectives' attention. *No*, she decided. She was safer to stay put and wait it out until they left.

Then she saw that Mojito had stopped washing her face and was now staring at Ellie from across the room. *Oh no, not again*, Ellie groaned silently.

The cat jumped off the sofa and trotted over to her. She stuck her nose behind the curtain and sniffed Ellie's ankles.

"*MIAOW!*" she said.

"*Go away!*" hissed Ellie under her breath.

She shot a look across the room, but thankfully both men still had their backs to her. They were deep in discussion and not paying any attention. Ellie glanced at the open screen door again. Maybe she should take the risk? In a way, Mojito had provided her with the perfect chance to attempt an escape. The cat's constant cries and disturbances had desensitized the detectives to random noises in the room. They were deliberately ignoring any sound now. Besides, if she remained here, she might be discovered soon anyway, especially if Mojito's curiosity with the curtains caught the detectives' attention.

Ellie took a deep breath and was just about to step out from behind the curtains when there was the sound of loud squawking and flapping outside. She turned and her heart sank to see Hemingway the scarlet macaw swoop down in a flurry of red feathers. He landed on the back of the lounge chair on the terrace and perched there.

The detectives looked up. The parrot noises had been too loud to ignore and now they stared at the bird in surprise.

"Jeez, this place is like a zoo," grumbled Carson.

"It's that stupid parrot," said the officer. "He nearly scared the hell out of me yesterday. Jumped out at me from behind a palm tree when I was down by the parking lot, then he laughed like a maniac."

The detective grinned. "Sounds like he has a sense of humor."

"*SQUAWK!*" said Hemingway.

He flapped his wings, then folded them against his back and leaned forward, tilting his head and peering through the screen door. Ellie swallowed nervously. Could the parrot see her?

Hemingway made a chattering sound, then he hooted like a train. Ellie tried to ignore him, hoping that if she kept very still, he would lose interest and fly off. Instead, the macaw bobbed up and down excitedly, and yelled:

"*PEEKABOO!*"

Ellie groaned inwardly. She shot a dirty look at the parrot. He seemed to be enjoying himself, watching her with a mischievous gleam in his eye.

"*PEEKABOO!*" he said again.

"What's it saying?" asked Carson, looking amused.

"I think it's saying 'peekaboo,'" said the officer.

"*PEEKABOO!*" shouted Hemingway, stretching his wings out, his long tail waving from side to side. He bobbed up and down again, looked straight at Ellie through the screen door, and croaked: "*I CAN SEE YOU!*"

Oh my God, Ellie groaned silently. This was awful! She wanted to throttle the bird. She tried to press herself even flatter against the wall as Detective Carson strolled over to the screen door.

"*I CAN SEE YOU!*" said Hemingway.

Carson chuckled. "I can see you too," he said.

He was turned slightly away from Ellie, so that his back was toward her, but he was so close that she could almost reach out and touch him. She saw the parrot eying her over the detective's shoulder.

"*LOOK OUT! BEHIND YOU!*" Hemingway screeched.

Ellie nearly fainted but Detective Carson roared with laughter.

"Know what? I like this bird. He's real funny," he

said.

Then he turned and walked back to the other side of the room, where he joined the officer once more in going through Lillian Fox's things. Ellie sagged against the wall in relief. *That was close!* She had been so sure that Carson would discover her. She could still feel her heart pounding in her chest.

Ellie glared at the parrot, then glanced back at the other side of the room. The men had their backs to her and were engrossed in their job. She eyed the open screen door thoughtfully. *I'm going to risk it*, she decided. She didn't dare stay in her hiding place any longer, in case the detectives discovered her, and even if they didn't, she didn't think her nerves could take any more strain!

Slowly, she eased out from behind the curtains and moved stealthily toward the gap leading out onto the terrace, all while keeping a wary eye on the men on the other side of the room.

Almost there... almost there...

Ellie was just stepping over the threshold and out onto the terrace when Hemingway began flapping his wings and shrieking with excitement.

"Shush! *Shush!*" hissed Ellie.

Then she froze as the two men whirled around to see what the commotion was about. She was caught in full view, standing half in, half out, of the sliding doors. Ellie's mind raced, then she had a wild idea. She spun around and pretended to be stepping *into* the villa, rather than out.

She let out a cry of relief and said: "Detective Carson! I heard the parrot screeching and yelling so I ran over to see what had happened! I thought someone was hurt or something."

The detective looked at her suspiciously and Ellie wondered if he was going to buy her story. Then he relaxed, obviously believing her.

"You came from next door? You sure moved quickly," he commented.

"Oh, I... erm... I was out on my terrace already when I happened to hear the noise," said Ellie airily. "I guess you didn't see me because of the privacy screen." She glanced at Hemingway who had calmed down slightly. "I'm glad it's just the parrot. He gave me a fright!"

"Yeah, that bird's a menace," grumbled the officer.

"Well, I'll leave you to your work now," said Ellie, giving the men a breezy smile and backing out of the living room.

For a moment, she thought Carson was going to stop her, then he nodded and returned to his work. With a huge sigh of relief, Ellie stepped out onto the terrace and pulled the doors shut behind her.

CHAPTER TWENTY-TWO

Ellie walked away from the sliding doors, trying to look as relaxed as possible. Hemingway hopped onto her shoulder as she walked past and rode along as she walked around the privacy screen and back over to her aunt's villa. The parrot began chattering again and bent to nibble strands of her hair from the side of her head.

"Hey, stop that—it tickles!" giggled Ellie, flinching away from the bird's beak. Then she remembered what had just happened next door and gave the macaw a mock glare. "I could kill you, you know! You nearly gave me away there, you sodding bird!"

"*YOU SODDING BIRD!*" repeated Hemingway with glee. "*YOU SODDING BIRD!*"

Oh no, Ellie groaned, putting her face in her hands. She had forgotten what she'd been told the other day, about how quickly Hemingway copied words and phrases from guests. She would have to watch her mouth around him.

Then she felt something furry brush her ankles and she looked down to see that the cat had followed them out of Lillian's villa as well. Mojito was now looking up at her with big green eyes.

"*MIAOW!*"

"You were just as bad," said Ellie, shaking a finger at Mojito. "The two of you nearly took five years off my life in there."

"*BAD KITTY!*" said the parrot, eyeing the cat with disapproval. "*BAD KITTY!*"

Ellie laughed in spite of herself. Mojito ignored the parrot. The two animals were obviously used to each other and, in fact, seemed to be competing for her attention. Mojito purred loudly and rubbed against Ellie's leg while the parrot reached out again to nibble on strands of her hair, as if grooming her.

"Ooh! Stop, Hemingway—that tickles!" giggled Ellie, wriggling and trying to get away from the parrot's attentions.

The macaw squawked and opened his wings for balance as she jiggled her shoulders, then he took off and flew to perch on the lounge chair on Aunt Olive's terrace. Mojito jumped up onto the chair to join him and settled down against the cushioned seat to wash herself. Ellie smiled and left the two of them to enjoy the sunset from the lounge, while she walked back around to the front of the villa. She was eager to get back inside, plug the USB drive into her laptop, and see what it contained.

When she got to the villa's front door, though, Ellie was surprised to find it open. She stepped inside, looking around apprehensively. *Did somebody try to break in?* she wondered. Then she saw what was parked in the hallway and laughed to herself. *No, not unless they were doing it with a huge trolley full of linen and cleaning equipment!*

Ellie guessed that Housekeeping was probably servicing her room. She heard a voice singing in the bathroom and went in to find Maria the maid busily polishing the taps at the sink. There was a caddy filled with squeegees, sponges, scrubbing brushes and other cleaning implements on the floor beside her.

"Oh!" Maria said in surprise as she saw Ellie in the mirror. She stopped singing and turned around. "Excuse me, ma'am, for coming in so late. I made up your bed this morning but I didn't get a chance to clean the rest of the suite properly. If you want me to come back later—"

"No, no, that's OK," said Ellie, waving a hand. "Please continue. I won't be in your way."

"I just need to dust things in the living area, then I'm done," said Maria, picking up the caddy.

Ellie followed her back out to the living room, eager for the maid to finish so she could have privacy to look at the USB drive. As she watched the woman work, Ellie reminded herself that Maria was still a suspect as well. She could vividly remember the way the maid had clenched her fists and said: "*I will kill any woman who tries to take you away from me!*" when she had been talking to Paolo.

Ellie noted that Maria was short and stocky, with strong, muscled arms. She certainly looked strong enough to hit a woman on the head and then push her into the pool. Was that what had happened? Had Maria come back to confront Lillian about Paolo and lost her temper? Had she hit Lillian in a jealous rage and then, worried about being found out, pushed the body into the swimming pool and run away?

But wouldn't I have heard something that night if there had been a fight next door? wondered Ellie. Then she admitted to herself that she'd had the TV turned on so loud, she probably wouldn't have heard anything.

On an impulse, she said in a chatty tone: "Maria... I suppose you met the woman next door? The one who was murdered? she asked.

Maria stiffened. "I cleaned her room but that is all," she said.

"What was she like? Was she nice? I heard that she was a really nice woman," said Ellie ingenuously. "One of the other resort staff told me that aside from being beautiful and sexy, Lillian Fox was also kind and generous and sweet and—"

"Who said that?" demanded Maria.

"Oh, the guy who makes cocktails at the Tiki Bar. I think his name's Paolo," said Ellie casually.

Maria's face flushed an angry red. "Paolo is wrong! Lillian Fox was not a nice woman at all! She thought of nobody but herself. She did terrible things and used people in cruel ways!"

"How do you know that?"

"Your aunt told me."

"My aunt?" Ellie reeled back in surprise. "Aunt Olive? She told you about Lillian?"

"Yes. Your aunt—she is the real 'nice woman.' She always cares about other writers, especially young ones, and wants to help them. I was cleaning here one morning—the morning before you arrived—and your aunt was working on her computer. Suddenly, I heard her say some curse words. She sounded very shocked and angry. I asked her what was wrong and she said she just learned some bad news about another writer."

"What kind of bad news?

Maria shrugged. "I don't know exactly. Your aunt didn't say. She just said, 'It was bad enough when Lillian was using fake names to leave bad reviews on other writers' books, but this is beyond belief!'" Maria looked up at Ellie. "You see what kind of woman Lillian Fox was?"

"So Lillian sabotaged other writers' books?" asked Ellie.

Maria nodded. "Your aunt also said she was a thief. She said she was going to speak to Lillian herself that evening."

Which is what Aunt Olive did, thought Ellie. That

must have been the "fight" that everyone had witnessed before the conference, the night before Ellie had arrived in Florida. The one that had made the police suspect her aunt.

Ellie wanted to ask Maria more, but the maid seemed in a hurry to leave. She finished her dusting, then grabbed the housekeeping cart and wheeled it out of the villa, shutting the front door firmly behind her.

Hmm... interesting, thought Ellie. Asking Maria about Lillian had obviously spooked her. In fact, the maid had been so desperate to get away from Ellie's questions, she had left a dusting cloth on one of the side tables. There was still a layer of dust on some of the shell ornaments beside the TV, so Maria had obviously rushed off without finishing her job.

She told me some interesting stuff about Lillian Fox though, thought Ellie. Then she remembered the USB drive she had found and drew it excitedly out of her pocket. Would this give her even more background information to solve the mystery of Lillian's murder?

A few minutes later, Ellie was sitting in front of her open laptop. She inserted the USB stick, double-clicked, and opened it. She was surprised that it hadn't been password-protected—Lillian Fox must have been very confident of her hiding place! It contained a folder labelled "Little Black Book." Ellie opened that, then stared at the huge list of sub-folders contained inside. Each was labelled, some with the names of people, others with initials or nicknames. There were so many folders that Ellie's heart sank. It would probably take her hours to go through them all. Then she zeroed in on a folder with a name she recognized: "Cheryl Jackson."

Ellie opened it. It held a single document, plus some images of Cheryl taken at various writer events. Ellie opened the document and scanned it quickly: it seemed to contain notes that Lillian Fox had made about her arch-rival, including slanderous gossip and harmful rumors. There were little comments inserted next to some of the information, where Lillian had written things like "Could be useful" or "Dig deeper" or "Spread on social media."

Ellie opened a few more folders with names she didn't recognize and saw that they contained similar documents. Lillian had obviously been gathering information about her peers—negative or sensitive information that she could use to control and manipulate and even destroy other peoples' careers and reputations. It was obvious, reading through the comments, that it wasn't just about money. Lillian wasn't trying to blackmail people for gain—she was more than successful enough herself from her own book sales. She just enjoyed power over others and watching them squirm. And she placed all the information she picked up in this digital version of a "little black book."

Ellie scrolled idly down the list of folders, then stopped as she spotted a folder with the name "Nancy—SPBR." She had a sudden hunch that

"SPBR" stood for "Sunset Palms Beach Resort," which meant that "Nancy" stood for Nancy Bertoli. Ellie clicked and opened the document. It only contained one line which read:

"Picked me up from the airport. Noticed that she—
"

That was it. Obviously, Lillian had been interrupted in the middle of writing this entry—perhaps someone had arrived at her villa or she had realized that she was late for something. Ellie looked up from the laptop screen in frustration. What had Lillian been about to write? Why did she have a folder on Nancy? She must have dug up something about the resort chauffeur—something she could use against the woman.

Oh my God... thought Ellie. She had never considered Nancy a suspect in the case but now, suddenly, she wondered if she had been completely blind!

CHAPTER TWENTY-THREE

Could Nancy be the murderer? Ellie wondered. The woman certainly had easy access: she was a member of the resort staff and nobody would question her hanging around the place. Her office was just by the Tiki Bar, within view of the Beach Villas Wing. She could have pretended to stay late in her office, watching Lillian's villa, and when the coast was clear and she saw the romance author return from the party, she could have sneaked across the pool area and gone in the villa via the sliding doors on the terrace.

Ellie drew a sharp breath. This meant that the shadowy figure that she had seen on the night of the murder could have been Nancy! Ellie had always assumed that it had been Paolo, because he worked by the pool, but it could just as easily have been the resort chauffeur. Nancy had a slim, athletic figure and short, cropped hair. From a distance, in the dark, she could easily have been mistaken for a man.

But what about the earring? Ellie wondered suddenly. She had been so sure that the earring she had found on Lillian's terrace had been dropped by the murderer. That was why she had suspected Ann. But now she recalled what Lynn had said at the gift shop the other day: *"They've been so popular. Beautiful but affordable. Even some of the resort staff have bought things from this line."* What if Nancy was one of the "resort staff" who had bought those shell earrings? Then she would have been the one who dropped one of the earrings that night, not Ann!

Oh my God, it all fits! thought Ellie. She rushed to the phone and pressed the internal number for the gift shop. Lynn answered after a moment.

"Hi Lynn—this is Ellie. I don't know if you remember me, but I was in your shop yesterday. I'm the English girl who was interested in the shell earrings?" she said breathlessly.

"Oh, sure, honey—of course I remember you," said Lynn. "You bought that darling little yellow bikini."

"Yes, that's right," said Ellie, impressed by the woman's memory. "Erm, Lynn—you said that some of the resort staff bought stuff from that line of seashell jewelry as well. Was one of them Nancy Bertoli? You know, the resort chauffeur?"

"Oh yeah, that's right. Barry from Marketing got a

pendant for his wife and Nancy got a pair of earrings. The same ones as your writer friend."

"Thanks so much!" said Ellie, and she hung up before Lynn could reply (or try to sell her anything else!).

She put the phone down and began pacing around the room. She knew that she ought to call the police immediately, but something held her back. For one thing... Ellie looked back down at the blank document on her laptop screen. She didn't actually know what information Lillian had had on Nancy. Without that, wasn't she just jumping to conclusions? She couldn't accuse Nancy just because the woman had bought some earrings! She needed to have a good motive. Besides, Ellie liked Nancy. She felt sorry for the woman. She remembered the way Nancy had looked that day when the hotel manager had threatened to fire her. She had seemed so desperate. The last thing Ellie wanted to do was add to the woman's troubles.

But that could also be the very reason that she's the murderer, Ellie reminded herself uneasily. Nancy had made it clear that she was willing to do anything to keep her job so she could support her son through college. So if someone like Lillian had threatened that in any way, wouldn't that be a motive for murder?

Ellie sighed and paced around the room again. She didn't know what to do. Then she glanced at the clock and suddenly remembered her dinner date.

I'll speak to Blake about it before I do anything, she

decided. He *had* offered to help and she was sure the handsome doctor would be able to help her think things through and decide what to do. Suddenly, she felt her spirits lifting. It was good to have a friend and not feel like she had to wrestle with everything on her own.

Shutting her laptop, Ellie hid the USB stick in her suitcase, then went to have a shower and wash her hair. Then she spent some time trying to decide what to wear. She wished again that she had brought some nicer outfits to Florida. Although the place that Blake had mentioned for dinner sounded fairly casual, she still wanted to look her best. At last, she settled on a simple white sundress with a wide sash belt. It was fairly old and she didn't have the tan yet to do it justice, but she thought the shape was more flattering to her figure than anything else she owned.

Ellie checked her appearance critically in the mirror and frowned. Her neck looked really bare. She went to her suitcase and dug out the small jewelry pouch she kept in there, then fished out a simple gold locket. She smiled as she looked down at it. This had been a sixteenth birthday gift from Aunt Olive and it was still one of her favorite pieces. She put it on and admired it in the mirror. The locket brought her aunt back to mind and Ellie felt a stab of worry and loneliness again. How she wished Aunt Olive were here! She sighed. A part of her felt a bit guilty going out to dinner, when she still didn't even know where Aunt Olive was. But she had already reported her aunt's disappearance to the local police and she didn't know what else she could do. Sitting alone in the villa all night wouldn't necessarily bring her aunt back any faster! Besides, her parents had told her not to worry...

I'll contact the British Embassy tomorrow, Ellie thought suddenly. *After all, Aunt Olive is a British citizen. If the local police can't help, then perhaps the embassy officials can.*

Feeling better, she started to hunt for her handbag. She was just going around the living room, looking behind the couch cushions, when she noticed a movement outside. She paused and looked out through the sliding doors. On the other side of the pool deck, just visible through the palm trees, was the Resort Travel & Transport Hut, where she had gone to speak to Nancy earlier that day. She could see a woman coming out of the hut and pulling the door shut behind her, then shouldering her handbag and striding away. It was Nancy and it looked like she had finished work for the day.

Ellie stood by the sliding doors, watching Nancy's figure getting smaller and smaller in the distance, until she disappeared around the corner. Ellie looked back at the hut. She hadn't seen Nancy lock the door. It seemed too good an opportunity to miss. She glanced at the clock on the wall again. There was still half an hour before she had to meet Blake.

Acting on an impulse, Ellie unlocked the sliding doors and stepped outside. Keeping to the shadows, she made her away across the pool deck to the Resort Travel & Transport Hut. Luckily, most of the pool area seemed to be deserted—even the Tiki Bar didn't have anyone hovering by the counter, waiting for a cocktail.

Ellie paused outside the hut and peered through the windows but the blinds were down and it was impossible to see in. She took a deep breath, opened the door, and stepped inside. The little waiting area outside, with the racks of tourist brochures, was lit by a small ceiling light, but Nancy's internal office was dark. Obviously, the hut had been left open so that guests could still come in after office hours to help themselves to brochures from the racks.

Ellie opened the door to Nancy's office and slipped inside. She didn't dare switch the lights on, but thankfully the office door had a glass panel set into it and there was enough light from the waiting area outside filtering in for her to see. She waited a moment for her eyes to acclimatize, then she moved swiftly over to the desk and began looking around. She didn't really know what she was searching for—it was just general snooping, really. But she hoped that she might find something which could give a clue as to what Lillian had been planning to write about Nancy in her digital "little black book."

Ellie opened the drawers beneath the desk and rummaged carefully through the piles of papers, stationery, and other office paraphernalia that she found. Nancy was a messy person and her drawers were disorganized and stuffed with a confusing variety of items. In the bottom drawer, Ellie found several flasks and thermoses. One of them looked identical to the flask that Nancy had been drinking from on the day she had picked up Ellie at the airport—the one which contained the resort chauffeur's beloved "health drink."

My God, she must really believe in the stuff, thought Ellie, eying the multiple flasks and thermoses. *What's in the health drink, anyway?* Idly, she picked one up and unscrewed the top, then raised it to her nose and sniffed. Instantly, she flinched back from the strong alcoholic fumes that wafted from the mouth of the flask.

Ellie lowered the flask and stared disbelievingly at it, then raised it to her nose and took another careful sniff. No, she hadn't been mistaken. Whatever "health drink" might have been in that flask, it sure contained a huge amount of strong liquor! Ellie hesitated, then carefully tilted the flask until she managed to pour a drop out onto her forefinger. She dabbed it on her tongue: just as she suspected, it was neat whiskey.

So this is Nancy's so-called "health drink!" Ellie thought back to the woman's headaches and bloodshot eyes, her struggle with the early morning light, and the pallor of her face... Suddenly she realized what those symptoms were: signs of a bad hangover. It explained the chauffeur's speeding and erratic driving, and the complaints of her hitting the posts at the resort entrance, plus the heavy smell of air freshener in the resort car and the woman's constant use of breath mints...

Nancy had a drinking problem.

Ellie stared at the flask in her hands. Was *this* the secret that Lillian had discovered? Yes, it must've been what she was murdered for! Nancy had been terrified that she was going to lose her job. The hotel manager had already warned her the other day that she was walking on thin ice. And Ellie remembered talking with the chauffeur on the drive back from the airport: Nancy had said, "There's nothing I wouldn't do to look after my boy."

Maybe Lillian had threatened to expose her alcoholism to the hotel management—just because she enjoyed watching people squirm. And Nancy had snapped. Desperate and terrified, she had decided to silence the romance author once and for all.

CHAPTER TWENTY-FOUR

A sound made Ellie jerk her head up and her heart skipped a beat when the door of the office opened. For a moment, she thought that Nancy had come back, but then she relaxed as she saw Ann Crosby standing in the doorway.

"Oh, Ann, it's you!" She breathed a sigh of relief, then beckoned urgently to the young woman. "Come in—quick!"

Ann looked startled but obediently came in and shut the door behind her.

"Ann, I've found Lillian's murderer!" Ellie said excitedly. "It's Nancy—the resort chauffeur!"

"Nancy? But why would she want to kill Lillian?"

"She's an alcoholic. I think Lillian must have found out about her drinking problem and threatened to expose her, and Nancy got desperate and killed her to silence her. I found Lillian's 'little black book,' you see."

"What?" Ann looked shocked. "What little black book?"

"It's not a real one—it's a digital version. It was in a USB stick that she had hidden in her room. Lillian had been keeping notes on everyone—nasty bits of gossip or rumors or just general information that she could use to take advantage of people. I have to admit, Lillian does sound like the most horrible person. She had dozens and dozens of folders on different people, with information on each of them."

"Wow... Did you look in all of them?"

Ellie shook her head. "I didn't have time. But I intend to later and I'm sure the police will be interested once I turn the USB drive over to them." She turned back to the open drawer where she had found the flasks. "I wonder if there might be more stuff in here. If I could find more evidence, then the police might—"

She broke off as something glinted at the bottom of the drawer. She reached in and fished it out, then stared in puzzlement at the pair of shell earrings she held in her hands. They were identical to the one that she'd found on Lillian's terrace beside the privacy screen.

"That's strange," Ellie murmured. "I thought Nancy was the one who dropped the earring on Lillian's terrace. But it looks like she has the full pair here, which means that she can't have dropped the earring that I found. So who dropped that earring then?"

Then it hit her. Slowly, Ellie raised her head and looked back up at the young, mousy woman standing next to her.

"It was you, wasn't it?" she whispered in horror. "You're the murderer! You lied when you said you didn't go around to Lillian's terrace and you lied when you told me that you still had the other one of your earrings—"

"Well, it wasn't really so much a lie as a bluff," said Ann. "It's funny—it's a scene you see a lot in books and movies, but you never expect it to work in real life! How many times have you read a novel or watched a film where someone goes, 'I can show you!' and the hero goes, 'Never mind, that's OK.' It's human nature, see? The minute I acted like I was willing to show you the earring, it made you think that I couldn't be guilty because I was being so open and forthcoming. I didn't have to actually show you anything to convince you of my innocence."

Ellie gave the other woman a look of disgust. "So was that shy author thing just an act too? I never pegged you as such a cold-blooded murderer."

"I'm not a cold-blooded murderer!" cried Ann. "I didn't intend to kill Lillian. I only went to her villa that night to talk to her, to confront her about what she did. I thought it would help to clear the air. I never meant to kill her but then..."

"But then what?"

Ann took a deep breath, then spoke in a calmer

voice. "I felt so angry, you know; so hurt and betrayed by what Lillian had done. I thought she would help me, not use me and take advantage of me! She'd made such a fuss on social media, talking up how she was going to mentor and help aspiring authors, so last year, when I saw her at one of the conferences, I went up to her and asked if I could show her the novel I'd been working on. I'd hoped that she might be able to give me some tips and I was so happy when she said yes. She asked me to send her my manuscript, so I emailed it to her."

Ellie had a bad feeling that she knew what was coming but she said nothing as Ann continued.

"I kept checking my email every day, hoping to see a reply from Lillian. I was too shy and nervous to chase her—I kept telling myself that a bestselling author like Lillian must be so busy and I had to be patient. But after six months with no word, I finally got the courage to email Lillian and ask her whether she'd had a chance to read my novel. She didn't reply. After another month, I tried again. Then again. I must have sent her half a dozen emails before she finally replied. It was a really short, curt response saying that she'd read it and it was rubbish and I should just scrap everything and start again."

Ann gave Ellie a bitter smile. "I was devastated, of course, but I told myself that I should have been grateful to get Lillian's expert opinion. So I shelved the manuscript and tried to move on, to start a new book. I didn't think about the whole episode again until a few days ago when I was on the plane flying to Florida. I started reading Lillian's latest book and I discovered that it was *my* story! Almost word for word! My characters, my setting, my plot... Lillian had stolen the whole thing and published it as her book!"

"Wow, that was pretty rotten of her," said Ellie.

"Yes, that woman was evil!" said Ann. "I felt so sick when I heard the other writers sucking up to Lillian before the conference and gushing about her new book—how wonderful the characters were, how amazing the plot was... They were *my* plot, *my* characters! It should have been my name on that book cover, not hers!"

Ann had tears in her eyes now and, in spite of the situation, Ellie felt sorry for her.

"I didn't mean to kill Lillian—I only meant to confront her that night, but she started laughing and jeering at me. She just stood there, twirling a cocktail umbrella around in her hands and mocking me! I felt something inside me snap." Ann clenched her fists. "When Lillian turned her back on me and walked out to the edge of the terrace, I thought—how easy it would be if she just fell in the pool and never came up again. She would never take advantage of another writer, never bully or manipulate anyone ever again... So I went up behind her and I raised the big hardback I'd been carrying and hit her on the head. It was so easy it was laughable. She staggered forward until she was near the edge of the pool, and

I just gave her a little push." Ann gave Ellie a defiant look. "So you see, it wasn't even as if I really killed her. She was still alive when she went in the water. She just drowned. It wasn't me who killed her—it was the water."

"What? What kind of convoluted logic is that?" cried Ellie. "You knew that if Lillian fell in with a head injury, she wouldn't be able to swim properly and would probably drown! By pushing her in, it was just as bad as stabbing her with a knife or something. And you just left, didn't you? You didn't regret what you'd done and try to pull her out again—"

"No, I don't regret what I did," snapped Ann. "Lillian was a witch and she deserved everything that she got! And yes, I left her there to drown. I didn't feel sorry at all. After all, accidents happen at resorts all the time. People drown. Too bad."

Ellie stared at the young woman in front of her. *I can't believe how I ever thought that Ann was shy and sweet. She's a complete psycho!* Then Ellie swallowed nervously as she realized something else: she was alone with the complete psycho.

CHAPTER TWENTY-FIVE

Ellie stole a glance at Ann again and wondered when the other woman would work out that she knew too much.

"Erm..." Ellie cleared her throat. "You know, I think you're right about Lillian. She really was a horrible woman and I'm sure everyone will be very sympathetic when they hear your story. I'm sure the police will understand and—"

"The police?" Ann frowned. "The police aren't going to know about this. No one can know."

"Well, I suppose we can discuss that later. Listen, why don't we go out and get some fresh air...?" Ellie tried to move around the desk toward the door, but Ann jumped in front of her.

"No!" she said, shaking her head vehemently. "I can't let you leave. You want to tell the police on me—

190

"

"I didn't say that. Look, the police are going to find out the truth eventually anyway. You might as well tell them your side of it first."

"They'll never believe me!" said Ann. "It'll be Lillian's word over mine and she was a bestselling author with a publisher who supported her whereas I'm nobody. They'll say that I was jealous of her, that I was vindictive and trying to steal some of her glory."

"But you could show them your original manuscript," Ellie pointed out.

"I can't. I threw it away!" snapped Ann. "I did exactly what Lillian told me to. The witch! She had it all planned out: get me to destroy the manuscript, and then she could easily claim that the story and characters were hers."

"You can still tell the police what really happened," said Ellie. "I'll back you up. I'll tell them all the things I've found about Lillian and how she really wasn't a nice person. I'm sure you're not the only person she used and abused. If we go through that USB stick, I'm sure we'll find others who—"

"No," said Ann, in an eerily calm voice. "No one can know about that USB stick. I'm sure Lillian's got me in a folder in there, somewhere. I don't want the police seeing that and linking anything back to me." She looked at Ellie. "And the police don't have to find out the truth. In fact, they never have to find out the truth... if you're dead."

"Uh... OK, let's not do anything hasty..." said

Ellie, trying to back away. She realized that she was wedged in a corner, with the desk on one side, a big filing cabinet on the other, and Ann in front of her. She looked around for something that she could use as a weapon, but there was nothing easily at hand.

"You can't do anything to me," she said desperately. "There's a resort full of people around us! People will hear. Someone will come."

Ann didn't seem to be listening. She was coming slowly forward, her eyes on Ellie's throat in a way that was really creepy. Then, without warning, she lunged.

Ellie screamed as she felt the other woman grab her and she began struggling like crazy. She felt Ann's fingers reach for her throat and gasped and choked as she felt the pressure on her windpipe. Desperately, she clawed at Ann's hands, then she reached wildly around and grabbed a fistful of Ann's hair in her own hand and yanked hard.

Ann gave a cry of pain and her hold loosened. It was only for a moment, but it was enough for Ellie to shove the other woman away from her. She heard Ann give a grunt of pain as she slammed against the side of the desk. Ellie pushed herself up and wriggled past the other woman. She staggered to the office door, wrenched it open, then fell into the waiting area outside. A second later she was stumbling out of the hut.

"Help!" Ellie shouted, but her voice came out weak and raspy. Ann's chokehold had obviously hurt her larynx and affected her voice. Ellie tried again. "Help! Help!"

But it was no use. Her voice was so faint that unless somebody was nearby, they wouldn't hear her. And to her dismay, she could see no one by the pool. Even the Tiki Bar was dark and empty.

Ellie turned and started stumbling away from the hut, but she hadn't gone a few steps when someone grabbed her from behind.

"No!" she cried as she went down with Ann on top of her.

The two of them wrestled and struggled, gasping and panting, until suddenly they were at the edge of the pool. Ellie wrenched free for a moment and tried to scream for help again but Ann grabbed her and yanked her close. They teetered over the edge, then fell into the water with a huge splash.

Ellie gasped as cold water closed over her head. She kicked frantically until she broke the surface again. Real panic set in. She couldn't swim! She thrashed around, coughing and spluttering.

"Help!" she gasped weakly. "I can't swim! Help me!"

Will anyone hear me? she wondered in despair. Then suddenly, to her surprise, she heard her own voice, shrilly magnified, crying:

"HELP! I CAN'T SWIM! HELP ME!"

She looked up and saw Hemingway perched on a palm tree next to the pool. He was flapping his wings and bouncing up and down, screaming and screeching, in between yelling for help in her voice.

He's mimicking me! thought Ellie.

Then she saw Ann surface next to her and reach out to grab her again.

"Nooo!" gasped Ellie, paddling frantically.

But she didn't really know how to coordinate her arms and legs to swim away. She could only thrash in a panic, kicking wildly and flailing her arms, as she felt Ann grab her around the waist. The world seemed to turn upside down. There was water in her eyes and her mouth, blinding her and choking her. There was a roar in her ears that was a mixture of her own harsh breathing, the sucking and splashing of water, and Hemingway's voice screeching: *"HELP! I CAN'T SWIM! HELP ME!"*

Then suddenly Ellie heard new sounds—cries, exclamations, shouts, the hubbub of many voices. She wrenched herself away from Ann and looked up to see that the parrot's ear-splitting cries had brought a whole crowd of people running to the pool. Blake Thornton was one of the first to arrive and the minute he saw Ellie in the water, he dived fully clothed into the pool.

"Ellie!" he shouted, swimming with swift, clean strokes toward her.

A second later, Ellie felt strong arms close around her and pull her away from Ann. She nearly cried with relief as she put her arms around Blake's neck and clung to him like a limpet. Cradling her gently, he swam to the edge of the pool, then lifted her out to the waiting arms of the resort security guards.

Ellie felt a thick towel being wrapped around her and she clutched it gratefully. She was shivering violently, even though the night was warm and the air was balmy. She saw Blake climb dripping out of the pool and give a few terse instructions to one of the resort staff before hurrying over to her.

"Are you all right?" he asked gently, leading her to one of the lounge chairs and helping her to sit down.

Ellie nodded, trying to stop her teeth chattering. "I... I d-don't know why I f-feel s-so c-cold," she said.

"It's probably the adrenalin. A form of shock," said Blake.

He hesitated, then sat down next to her and put his arm around her. Ellie leaned gratefully into his chest, savoring the strength and warmth of his body.

'Here," said Blake as one of the resort staff came by and handed a glass to him. He gave it to Ellie. "Drink some of this. It will warm you up."

Ellie took a sip, then made a face. "What is it?"

"Brandy." Blake smiled at her. "An old remedy but it works."

Ellie obediently took another few sips and was surprised to find that she did feel a warmth begin to permeate her body. The shivering subsided and her teeth stopped chattering. She looked up, feeling more like herself again, and noticed that they had also pulled Ann out of the pool. The other woman had been wrapped in a towel too and was huddled by the edge of the water, surrounded by people.

"What's going on?" demanded Mr. Anderson the hotel manager, pushing his way out of the crowd. "What happened here?"

Ellie took a deep breath, then pointed to Ann. "She tried to kill me."

There were gasps and cries of disbelief from the crowd.

"I'm... I'm sorry?" said Mr. Anderson, looking at Ellie incredulously. "Ma'am, are you accusing this lady of attempted murder?"

"Yes," said Ellie. "She wanted to kill me because I knew too much and she didn't want me to go to the police with the truth."

"What truth?" said Mr. Anderson, looking completely bewildered.

"That she's the one who murdered Lillian Fox."

There were more gasps and cries and all heads turned to look at Ann. For a moment, Ellie thought the writer was going to deny everything. Then Ann took a step forward and lifted her chin, looking at everybody defiantly.

"Yeah, I admit it. It was me. And you know what? I don't regret it! Lillian was a horrible, evil woman and she deserved to die!" Ann said. Then suddenly she gave a twisted smile and added: "And you know what I'm going to do with my time in prison? I'm going to write *my* account. I bet the publishers will line up to give me a deal for my side of the story. Maybe I'll have a bestselling book at last, huh?"

CHAPTER TWENTY-SIX

"Oh yes, I was always suspicious about Ann Crosby. I've got great instincts, you see, and I understand people. It comes from being a romance writer, especially one who has been as successful as I have. I could always tell that there was something off about that girl."

Ellie wanted to roll her eyes as she watched Cheryl Jackson standing in the resort lobby, basking in the attention of a crowd of reporters and cameramen.

"So you knew that Ann had committed the murder?" asked Ted Baxter, pen poised over his pad.

"Like I said, I had strong suspicions," said Cheryl coyly. "But, of course, you can't just go around accusing people without proof. I had to do some sleuthing first."

"Sleuthing? So do you have experience with

detective work, Ms. Jackson?" asked another reporter.

"Well, not exactly, but being a writer, I'm excellent at research and I always take it very seriously for my books," said Cheryl. "For example, when I wanted to include a scene featuring a sleeping pill in my current book, I went to a real doctor to ask about its effects. I didn't just rely on Googling."

"Ms. Jackson, did you help the police with their investigation?" asked another reporter, thrusting a microphone at her.

Cheryl fluffed her hair. "Oh, well, Detective Carson did interview me for a long time and I'm sure he found my insights *very* helpful..."

Ellie turned and walked out of the lobby. She couldn't stand listening to Cheryl any longer. In her own way, the woman was just as obnoxious! Still, that comment about the sleeping pills solved the mystery of why Cheryl had been asking Blake for the information.

Ellie walked past the pool deck and paused for a moment, eying the lounge chairs there, then she turned and kept walking, taking the path that led off the landscaped grounds, through the dunes, and out onto the beach. She approached the row of cabanas laid out in a line facing the water. She was pleased to see that one was free and showed the attendant her bracelet before climbing in and making herself comfortable. There was a menu tucked against one of the cushions and Ellie ordered herself a cocktail and a snack. She was delighted when the waiter who brought her order several minutes later turned out to be a smiling man she recognized.

"Sol! How nice to see you! How have you been?" she asked.

"Oh, not bad, not bad," he said. "How about you, ma'am?"

"Oh please—call me Ellie," she begged him. "Honestly, I'm beginning to feel like a ninety-year old monarch!"

Sol laughed. "All right, Ellie. As long as Mr. Anderson doesn't hear me. He's got strict ideas, you know, about how we speak to the guests, and he's a real stickler for the rules!" He indicated the tray that he had brought for her. "I got your piña colada here and the Cuban sandwich you ordered, and I included a little something extra." He pointed to a small bowl of mixed nuts. "Our own special blend. Be careful—it's spicy!"

"Looks delicious! Thanks!"

After he left, Ellie devoured the sandwich, then tried the nuts. Whew! *Sol was right—they're spicy! And also really addictive!* Ellie found herself reaching for another and another, then sipping her drink thirstily.

She stretched out on the cabana and leaned back against the cushions with a sigh. The sun was warm on her face, the view of the beach was stunning, she had a cocktail in one hand, a bowl of delicious snacks at her elbow, and the rest of the day ahead of her to lounge around or explore the delights of one of the best resorts in Florida... She should have been happy, she should have been enjoying herself, but she couldn't. Because even though Lillian Fox's murderer was safely in police custody and the murder case was solved, the mystery of Aunt Olive's disappearance still remained.

Last night, after getting Ellie's statement and learning all the information she had uncovered about Lillian's murder, Detective Carson had been grudgingly impressed and admitted that her detective skills were "not bad." He had also apologized for suspecting her aunt and promised to continue looking for Aunt Olive as a "missing persons" case.

"Just to warn you, though—I've worked quite a few missing persons cases and we usually don't get a result," he'd said. "Sometimes people just want to disappear from their lives. It happens. So don't be surprised if your aunt never turns up. She might not want to be found."

But Ellie hadn't believed him. She was sure that Aunt Olive would never just disappear from her life without even a goodbye. She hoped that what her mother and father had said was true—that it was just her aunt being her usual self and taking off on some impulsive trip.

It's only been three days, really, since Aunt Olive was last seen, Ellie reminded herself. It was only because so much had happened in the last couple of days that it felt longer.

A loud raucous cry interrupted her thoughts and she looked up to see a large red bird swooping across the beach.

"Hey Hemingway!" called Ellie, smiling and waving at the parrot.

The scarlet macaw swerved in midair and flapped his huge wings, coming to land on the roof of Ellie's cabana.

"*PEEKABOO!*" he said, tilting his head to eye her from above. Then his pupils dilated as he spotted the bowl of mixed nuts next to her.

"*WANNA NUT?*" he shouted, bobbing up and down.

Ellie laughed. "All right, Hemingway. I suppose you've earned it. You saved my life, you know. If you hadn't started shouting for help, I think I would have probably drowned."

She scooped up a handful of nuts from the bowl and offered them to the macaw. "Be careful though. They're hot!"

Hemingway climbed slowly down the side of the cabana, using his beak and claws, then waddled across the cushioned seat to her and peered at the pile of nuts in her palm. Delicately, he fished out a Brazil nut with his beak, held it in one claw, and expertly cracked it. Ellie smiled as she watched him enjoy the nut. He didn't seem to mind the spicy flavor at all. In fact, he seemed to love it, eagerly reaching for another nut and another.

Then Ellie heard another familiar voice:

"*MIAOW!*"

She leaned out and peered over the side of the cabana to see Mojito the resort cat standing there on the sand, looking up at her.

"You too?" Ellie said with a chuckle. "Do you guys always go everywhere together? Well, all right, come on up! Plenty of room in here."

The cat needed no second invitation. She jumped up and joined Ellie on the cabana cushions, kneading and purring happily. Ellie reached out absentmindedly to pat Mojito and was surprised to find it strangely soothing. Even her worries about her aunt seemed to recede slightly as she stroked the silky, soft fur. She looked down, admiring the colors and patterns in the cat's pelt. It was amazing how Mojito managed to keep herself so sleek and clean, despite wandering everywhere on the resort and the beach. There wasn't a grain of sand in sight amongst the thick fur.

Then a shout made Ellie look up. Several people were pointing to a powerful boat which had dropped anchor in the deeper water just off the beach in front of the resort. As Ellie watched, two figures climbed over the side and splashed into the water, then began swimming toward the beach.

She stared, hardly daring to believe her eyes. The figures got closer, wading now through the shallower water closer to the beach. Ellie sat upright.

Is that? Oh my God... it is! It's Aunt Olive!

Ellie sprang up off the cabana, causing Hemingway to flap his wings and screech in alarm. She began running across the sand, toward the edge of the water.

"Aunt Olive! Aunt Olive, I can't believe it's you!" Ellie cried.

The shorter of the two figures stopped wading and shaded her eyes, peering up the beach.

"Ellie? Oh my goodness, poppet—you're here in Florida?" Aunt Olive beamed. "I thought you weren't coming until next week!"

She waded out of the water just as Ellie reached her and they hugged each other tightly.

"Aunt Olive, where have you been? I was so worried about you!" cried Ellie, letting go at last and leaning back to look at her aunt.

Olive Goldberg was a trim woman in her mid-sixties, with curly grey hair and a mischievous twinkle in her eyes. She was wearing a bright pink swimsuit under a boho-style top and a pair of Bermuda shorts more suited to a woman half her age, and had matching bright pink lipstick on her lips.

"Worried? About me?" Aunt Olive looked at her niece quizzically. "Whatever for?"

"Because you just disappeared!" said Ellie. "You just left without telling anyone anything and I arrived and your room was empty... You didn't even take your handbag or your clothes! Your bed wasn't slept in, and nobody had seen you since the night before the conference. It was like a missing persons case and—"

"Missing persons? What fiddle-faddle!" said Aunt Olive, laughing. "Anyone would think I'd been kidnapped by pirates, the way you're carrying on, dear. I just decided to go on an impromptu trip. I'm here on vacation. I can do what I like. Why should that be strange?"

"But you're missing the writers' conference!" said Ellie. "Isn't that what you came to the Sunset Palms Beach Resort for?"

"Oh, that." Aunt Olive gave a dismissive wave. "I've been to the NRWS conference dozens of times. It's always the same gossip and drama. I knew I wouldn't miss anything if I skipped a few days."

"You could have at least left a note!"

"Why?" asked Aunt Olive innocently. "I didn't think you were arriving until next week and there's no one else here that I'm accountable to."

"What about the other writers?"

Aunt Olive shrugged carelessly. "Oh, they wouldn't miss me. Besides, this isn't school, you know. We're all adults and we can come and go as we please. Really, dear, I don't know why you're making such a fuss."

Ellie sighed. She supposed that her aunt was right—if she hadn't arrived in Florida early, nobody would probably have even commented on Aunt Olive's absence. Perhaps one or two of her writer friends might have noticed it, but they would probably have shrugged it off and went about their own business, convinced that they would meet up with Olive eventually at some talk or social event.

"I hope you didn't really report me as a missing person," said Aunt Olive, pursing her lips. "The last thing I want to do is talk to the police."

"Oh. Erm... well, I'm afraid you're not going to be able to avoid that," said Ellie ruefully. "Although at least they won't be questioning you as a potential murder suspect."

"What? A murder?" Aunt Olive looked at Ellie incredulously. "Who's been murdered?"

"Lillian Fox."

"Great gibbons!" exclaimed Aunt Olive. "How on earth did Lillian get herself murdered?"

Ellie told her aunt everything that had happened in the last few days. "So you can see why the police were suspicious about you, given your history with Lillian," she said as she finished.

"Did *you* believe that I could be involved?" asked Aunt Olive with a teasing look.

"No, of course not! But you can see why I was confused and worried, especially when Nancy told me that you were asking whether you could hire a fast boat to make a getaway directly from the beach!"

Aunt Olive chuckled. "Ah yes. It was just for book research, dear. I'm thinking of setting my next book in a resort like this one, and I needed to know if a plot idea I had could work. Of course, when Nancy gave me Earl's details, I had no idea what a sexy old fox he would turn out to be..." She glanced at the man beside her with a coy smile.

For the first time, Ellie turned to look properly at the man standing next to her aunt. She recognized Earl Stone from his picture on the pamphlet, although he looked even more ruggedly handsome in real life. With his long grey hair pulled back in a low ponytail, his blue eyes narrowed against the sun, and his muscled chest and arms, it was hard to believe that Earl was in his sixties. He nodded hello to her and Ellie gave him a cautious smile in return, then she said to her aunt:

"So... erm... you've been with Earl this whole time?"

Aunt Olive giggled. "Yes! We've been out on the water. I went to see Earl, to ask him some research questions, and he was just casting off for a trip so he asked me if I wanted to come with... and I said yes!"

"What—just like that?" said Ellie in disbelief. "But... but you barely know him!" She lowered her voice. "What if he had been a criminal or something?"

"Oh, for goodness' sake—you sound like your father!" said Aunt Olive, rolling her eyes. "I could tell that Earl was a good person. There are some things you can just *feel*. Besides, I'd done some research on him; he's well known in the area and he had many glowing testimonials online."

"Reviews can be faked," muttered Ellie. "And I can't believe you just took off without coming back to your room to get extra clothes or toiletries or anything!"

Aunt Olive tutted. "That's what being spontaneous is all about, poppet! Just grabbing life with both hands when an opportunity presents itself and jumping in! No questions, no worrying about what you *ought* to be doing or what everyone expects." She laughed again and whooped: "I've been in these same clothes for three days—can you imagine? Three days! And we've been living off fish and drinking beer and sleeping naked on deck... It's been wild!"

Ellie looked at her aunt with a mixture of exasperation and reluctant admiration. So her parents had been right about Aunt Olive after all. Her disappearance had been nothing more sinister than an impromptu boat trip. And Detective Carson had been right too when he suggested that her aunt had met someone. She was also beginning to see why her parents found Aunt Olive so infuriating. She was completely careless and carefree, jumping impulsively into things without giving any thought to those she might be worrying.

"Well, I gotta get going," drawled Earl, making a gesture as if he were tipping an imaginary hat. "Nice to meet you, Ellie. I'll see you around, Olive—"

"Oh no, Earl! You've got to come into the resort and have a drink first," exclaimed Aunt Olive.

She linked her arm in his and began leading the way across the sand, back toward the resort. Ellie followed. They crossed the beach and walked over the dunes and into the landscaped grounds which surrounded the pool. Aunt Olive immediately made a beeline for the Tiki Bar, dragging Earl with her. Ellie hung back, not sure she wanted to watch her aunt flirting with Earl. *For goodness' sake, she's sixty-four!* thought Ellie. Then she shook her head in resignation and smiled to herself. Still, she had to admit that it was nice to have Aunt Olive back and to finally be able to relax and not worry anymore.

CHAPTER TWENTY-SEVEN

"I'm glad to see you looking so happy. I guess you didn't suffer any ill effects from yesterday's traumatic experience?"

Ellie turned at the sound of the familiar baritone and found Blake standing behind her. He was smiling at her, his brown eyes warm.

"Oh Blake!" she cried. "You're not going to believe it—my aunt's turned up!" She pointed to Aunt Olive in the distance, then told him the outrageous reason for her aunt's absence.

"I can't believe she did that," Ellie said, shaking her head as she finished. "Here I was thinking that she had been kidnapped or worse, and all along, she was enjoying some kind of... of personal *Love Boat* experience!"

Blake laughed, looking across at Aunt Olive on the

other side of the pool. "Your aunt sounds like quite the character. I look forward to meeting her in person."

"Oh, I'm sure she'd like to meet you too. She's a terrible flirt, Aunt Olive, and she's always had an eye for hunky young men... erm, I mean—" Ellie broke off, flushing and horrified at what she had just said. She stammered, "Sorry, I don't know why I said that... I mean, not that you're not hunky... but... erm—"

Blake grinned. "Oh, please, don't apologize. My head was just expanding nicely."

"Uh... so are you having a day off today?" asked Ellie, desperate to change the subject. "I thought you'd be at your clinic."

"I took some time out to go downtown with Nancy. I wanted to take her to see a colleague of mine and I knew she would never go on her own."

"Oh." Ellie hesitated. She wanted to tell Blake about Nancy's drinking problem, but somehow she also felt like she was betraying the woman. *Still, I'm ultimately helping her by speaking up*, Ellie reminded herself.

"Erm... you know, Nancy seems to like her drink. I mean... *really* like it," she said, giving Blake a meaningful look. "I wonder if maybe... erm... her health issues might be related?"

Blake looked at her silently for a moment, then he said in a neutral voice: "My colleague is a psychologist who specializes in alcoholism."

Ellie drew her breath in sharply. "So you knew!"

"I'd suspected for some time," Blake admitted. "But of course, like many alcoholics, the biggest issue Nancy had was denial. Getting her to admit she had a problem was the toughest step. I'm glad she agreed to go with me today—I think now she'll be able to get the help that she needs."

"I'm so glad!" said Ellie. "I really like Nancy and I'd been struggling with myself, wondering whether to tell someone my suspicions. I wanted her to get help but it also felt like a sort of betrayal—like me sticking my nose in something that wasn't my business, you know? After all, Nancy isn't a close friend or family or anything, and now that I know she wasn't involved in the murder, I didn't really have any reason to expose her secret, especially as I knew that it might make her lose her job."

"Well, I've spoken to Mr. Anderson about that," said Blake. "And he's agreed to let Nancy keep her job on compassionate grounds. She's been given some time off to sort things out and prove that she's in control of her addiction."

Ellie gave him a look of glowing admiration. "You've sorted everything wonderfully."

Now it was Blake's turn to look embarrassed. He rubbed his neck and hastily changed the subject. "So... are you looking forward to a little sightseeing now?"

"Oooh, yes!" said Ellie. "I can't wait to really start enjoying Florida! I mean, I've seen some pretty wonderful stuff already and the resort has been amazing, but it was all a bit overshadowed, you know, by Lillian's murder and Aunt Olive's disappearance. Whereas now..." Ellie stretched her arms above her head and tilted her head back, closing her eyes and enjoying the warmth of the sun on her face. "Now, I get to really start my vacation! No more dead bodies, no more mysteries, no more detective work; just a nice, peaceful time where nothing weird happens—"

"I wouldn't be so sure about that. Some people say Florida is the definition of where weird stuff happens," said Blake, chuckling. "The Sunshine State can be full of surprises."

"Well, from now on, I'm just going to be a boring tourist," insisted Ellie. "I can't wait to see some of the local attractions, do some shopping, check out the resort facilities... ooh, and I'd love to try some watersports; kayaking and paddle boarding look like such fun! And the banana boat too! Although I'm not sure if I should, because I can't swim—"

"Wait," Blake interrupted. "You really can't swim?"

"Yes. That's why I was screaming for help in the pool last night," said Ellie, putting on a "*duh!*" expression.

"I thought you were just panicking."

"I *was*—because I can't swim."

Blake raised an eyebrow. "You're really telling me that you've come to a beach resort in Florida and you can't swim?"

"Yup," said Ellie with a rueful smile.

"Well, we'd better fix that right away."

"What d'you mean?"

"I think what you need is a swimming lesson, Miss Bishop," said Blake, grinning. "And I know just the doctor to help you with that."

Ellie stared at him, her thoughts churning. She knew that she should put Blake off, but somehow she couldn't seem to find the words. *The new year is still weeks away*, she told herself. *I won't be leaving Florida for ages yet... what's wrong with a little swimming lesson?*

Ellie took a deep breath and smiled at Blake. "It's a date."

THE END

ABOUT THE AUTHOR

USA Today bestselling author H.Y. Hanna writes fun cozy mysteries filled with clever puzzles, lots of humor, quirky characters - and cats with big personalities! She is known for bringing wonderful settings to life, whether it's the historic city of Oxford, the beautiful English Cotswolds or the sunny beaches of coastal Florida.

After graduating from Oxford University, Hsin-Yi tried her hand at a variety of jobs, including advertising, modelling, teaching English, dog training and marketing... before returning to her first love: writing. She worked as a freelance writer for several years and has won awards for her novels, poetry, short stories and journalism.

A globe-trotter all her life, Hsin-Yi has lived in a variety of cultures, from Dubai to Auckland, London to New Jersey, but is now happily settled in Perth, Western Australia, with her husband and a rescue kitty named Muesli. You can learn more about her and her books at: www.hyhanna.com.: www.hyhanna.com

Join her Readers' Club Newsletter to get updates on new releases, exclusive giveaways and other book news!

https://www.hyhanna.com/newsletter

ACKNOWLEDGEMENTS

I'm incredibly grateful to my beta readers, Kathleen Costa and Connie Leap, for their huge help in the development of this new series. They've been invaluable in providing me with insights into American culture and habits, which are not so familiar to me, and for helping me check accuracy of details about the location. I also really appreciated their support and encouragement when I was struggling with the usual doubts and worries that comes with launching a new series!

I'm very lucky also that in his youth, my editor used to work in a Florida resort very similar to the one featured in my story and so had first-hand knowledge and experience of the setting—and endless patience with my questions! Thanks also to my assistant Erin for giving me another American perspective and for helping me stay organized and taking the load off, so I could concentrate on writing.

Last but not least, I'm eternally thankful to have my amazing husband by my side. He is the most understanding, supportive and loving partner any author could ask for, and a man in a million.